FIRST FRIDAY IN DECEMBER

S.J. Thompson

Copyright © 2022 S.J. Thompson

All rights reserved.

ISBN: 9798844446283

To my beloved husband.

First Friday in December

The First Year
      The Sinful Priest
      How to Avoid a Scandal
      Wearing the Budget of a New Car
      Champagne or Mulled Wine?
      Forty Going on Sixty
      The 'Not So Social' Social Event

The Second Year
      Behind the Green Door
      The Art of Being a Leading Lady
      Feeling Like a Bond Girl
      Nipples on a Front Page
      To Write a Love Song
      The Manhood Test
      Flirting with an Employee
      Wet Feet in Boots

The Third Year
      The Perfect Facades
      Perfect or Psycho?
      The Advantage of London's Black Cabs
      The Perks of Newfound Fame
      Gown in a Paper Bag
      Not a Walk in the Park
      The Deal Breaker

The Fourth Year
> The Postcard
> The Return of the Shawl
> The Common English Name
> The Snowflake Catching
> The Piano Bar
> The Text from Harald

The First Year

The Sinful Priest

Christine woke up suddenly to the alarm.

It was still very dark. It was December in Oslo, and the sun wouldn't rise until closer to ten. It was as hard to get up at five thirty in the morning as it was at eight o'clock, so Christine thought she might as well get something done before the short day was over. She had never hit the snooze button, at least not after she had started this job.

Well rested, she lifted her head from her pillow. The sharp smell of alcohol hit her. She instantly knew that Henrik was lying next to her, even though she couldn't remember noticing him coming to bed. He had been away for so many weeks, but she hadn't managed to stay awake until he got home. Christine didn't turn on the light, she just tried quietly to get out of bed without waking him up. His face was half way covered by his pillow, the rest was hiding behind his long, blond curls.

Christine snuck out to the kitchen and turned on her small coffee maker which was neatly stuffed inside one of the cabinets. Henrik had bought a fancy beast of an espresso machine, but she had never learnt to use it properly. She had no time to ground coffee, set the steam and have this process every morning. For her quick morning routine, she was happy with her speedy little coffee maker.

While the coffee maker started to make some noise, Christine looked around and noticed an open pizza box on the large marble countertop. A rather large piece was lying face down on the floor. She lifted the piece up carefully, but the tomato sauce had already left a mark on the oak floor. Henrik had fallen in love with these scrubbed floorboards after he had visited a friend's castle or something in Denmark somewhere. Afterwards, he had insisted on having the same floors, although it was recommended that they were cleaned properly twice a week. Henrik had never cleaned anything but himself in his whole life, so he didn't see this as a problem at all.

Christine tried to remove the stain but had to give up rather quickly, there was no time for that now. On her way to the bathroom, she started to text the cleaning lady instead.

Christine looked up on the painting that was hanging over the kitchen counter. It was a massive oil painting Henrik had bought at a gallery in Milan, and he had brought it home with him without showing it to Christine. Henrik liked to collect art, but this piece in particular was far from Christine's taste. Christine thought at first it was an old painting from centuries ago because of the technique. It was very detailed and done in oil paint, a gloomy portrait of a catholic priest whose face filled almost the whole canvas. His eyes were fiercely green and the intensity made Christine feel like he was staring at her wherever she was in the room. If the painting was carefully examined, you would notice a rather large tattoo, that at first seemed like a shadow on the priest's neck. Henrik once said to her: 'it's traces of a past, sinful life'.

Christine was not religious, but felt as if the painting was judging her every time she passed. When Christine told Henrik that she didn't like to have a priest judging her every time she walked by, Henrik had told her that she should see the painting as a reminder that even the most decent people are sinners.

Christine took the little cup of espresso with her into the

bathroom, draining it on her way, before putting it down on the side of the sink.

She showered quickly and put on a little bit of makeup. She felt like she had no idea how to apply it properly, and therefore stayed to her simple routine. Her fair skin only needed a little blush to look fresh, and her light blue eyes only needed a bit of mascara. She quickly put her dark brown hair into a simple chignon, a way of covering up the fact that she couldn't be bothered to wash her hair that often.

Christine then hurried quietly through the bedroom, and into the walk-in-closet. She put on her daily winter uniform of dark pants and a warm sweater. The rest of the year she lived in plain white shirts, but in winter the office had a terrible draught.

Afterwards, Christine sat down beside Henrik. She put her face close to his and stroked his forehead with her hand. Although his golden tan looked great, his blond locks were sweaty and smelled of cigarettes. He was breathing heavily, and didn't notice her close presence at all.

She gently kissed his forehead. 'I love you,' she whispered.

Henrik usually mumbled something back, but this morning there was no answer from him at all.

Before Christine went out the door, she wrote a note to Henrik in huge letters, and put it on the table in the hall. *Remember to pick up your tails at the cleaners! C* it said.

He'll probably forget it, she thought, as she put on her wool coat, tied the belt and wrapped her scarf around her neck. Usually, it was Christine who took care of errands like that, but she had told Henrik that she wouldn't have time today. She had only forty minutes from the last meeting until she had to be ready in the office foyer before tonights dinner.

Locking the apartment door, Christine ran down the big circular stairs. The sound of her steps rung through the spacious foyer. When they first moved in, Christine had tried to not wake up the whole building with her morning run down the stairs. She had quickly realised that there was no way of getting up or down without making a lot of noise, since the stairs was of stone and the room felt like it had the same acoustic properties like a church. Christine was usually out the door and looking forward to her next cup of coffee before any neighbours had even put on the hot water, as there was no creaking from the old pipes.

Outside, it was still as dark as at midnight, except for a few streetlights that lit up the classical Frogner facades. They were all in greyscale, as it was too dark to see their colours. Christine had always thought Frogner was reminiscent of Paris, especially at this hour. The similar architecture, the cobblestone streets, a dozen different shades of grey, were transformed by the dusting of dry snow that blew easily away when cars drove by.

Christine felt the cold bite her cheeks as soon as she came outside. The cold winter air was clear, and she thought the first two breaths were quite refreshing to breathe in. When she exhaled, the streetlights illuminated the clouds that came out of her mouth. She dug her hands in her pockets and found both her hat and her shearling mittens, and put them on. Her regular café was not too far away, just across the street, but she couldn't get there soon enough.

*

When she closed the door behind her at her regular café, she felt relieved to escape the cold. She ordered a large cup of coffee, which she could hear was still brewing. Every morning, she sat down in the same corner, and today was no different.

Still cold, Christine draped her coat over her shoulders. Christine then grabbed a big pile of work papers from her big tote bag. Although she had received them by email, she liked to go through them on paper. She read them calmly as part of her morning routine, although they made her bag a lot heavier than necessary.

Christine was deep in thought when she heard the bell ring.

The bell on the door felt as old as the heavy oak door. She tried to say focused and didn't lift her head, but she couldn't help overhearing the conversation. The voice of the male customer was too interesting.

'Ahh, yes, hello. How are you? Extremely cold today, isn't it? Feels like I'm freezing my nose off. Anyway, is it possible to get a cup of coffee, please?' Christine could hear the customer rub his palms together and blow on his fingers to warm them. He was speaking with a perfect English accent, a posh and deep but ultimately pleasant voice. He sounded like he was in a good mood, which was not something Christine at all associated with a posh Englishman. She usually found them rather snooty and condescending, but this voice wasn't like that at all. There were rarely anyone in the café before Christine in the morning, and never anyone with such an accent. Christine kept her head deep down in her papers - but, her focus was not on her papers any longer.

'Was that all?' The teenage girl mumbled.

'Yes.. No wait, I'll go for a cinnamon bun, please. I had one yesterday, and they were to die for. I think it's the best cinnamon buns in the world. I'm addicted.'

'Eating in or to go?' the girl said slowly. Christine was amazed that it could take the girl such a long time to say such a short sentence.

'To go, please,' the man replied. 'No, wait, I'll have it here instead. I'm not your first customer, I can see.' Christine noticed his voice had begun to calm down. '..And here I thought I deserved a medal for being here before seven.'

Christine couldn't help but smile a little. She thought it was quite sweet that someone had actually tried to chat with the bored girl. She herself had tried so many times herself, but to no avail. While Christine was not at all great at small talk, she knew she was at least better than that girl. She found it quite strange that someone had thought it was even a good idea to give the girl a job - she couldn't have been very talkative in the interview, and she never appeared to be an efficient employee.

Christine tried to continue with her reading, something she had pretended to be doing all along. Finally, she couldn't help herself, she had to have a quick look at him.

He was facing her, sitting at the table on the other side of the room. He was more handsome than she had imagined. He had dark brown hair, which was slightly wavy, but far from curls longer. He wasn't as pale as she had imagined, but it was a far cry from Henrik's golden glow. He was wearing round glasses with tortoiseshell rims, and was smartly dressed in a wool blazer and sweater. Beside him on the bench lay his wool overcoat, neatly folded. He was reading something, like she was.

To Christine, he looked proper and polite. Polite was not the same as nice, she had once learned, but this guy seemed genuine when he spoke, at least.

She glanced at her watch. She had completely forgotten to watch the time! She had overheard in the conversation that it was before seven, but now it was five minutes past, and she needed to be ready for a conference call at seven-thirty.

Christine got up quickly and put on her coat without taking the time to close it, or even putting her papers in her bag. She left the café with her papers under her right arm, and her tote bag in the other.

As she rushed past the man, Christine noticed out of the corner of her eye that he looked at her, but she kept her eyes on the door.

Outside it was still dark, and the cold hit her the moment she was stepped through the door. It was another reason to get to the office as soon as possible.

Christine rushed into the street, but while putting her foot down on the pavement, she suddenly slipped. She felt like she was turned upside down, with both her feet in the air, screaming as she fell. She saw the papers fly up into the air.

Christine had been so stressed that she had forgotten how slippery cobblestone streets could be. There had obviously been a thin layer of ice on them. She was amazed that her big scarf had saved her head from crashing onto the cobblestones, it was her bum that had taken the hit and she could already feel a bit of pain in her lower back. As she lifted her upper body and pulled her arms behind her, she looked around. Her documents laid scattered in the street. There were no cars around, fortunately. She sighed with relief.

While she was laying there, flat out on the ground, Christine could hear the doorbell of the café ring.

'Are you all right, miss?' The man from the café was right behind her. He must have heard her scream and had run out right behind her. Christine turned her head towards him. He was now on his knees next to her.

"Miss?"

Christine looked straight into a pair of very big, dark brown eyes, exaggerated by his glasses. They were brown, but almost grey at the centre. He had a straight, rather long nose, and she thought she could spot a couple of freckles. He was newly shaved, he was probably one of those who had to shave several times a day to not grow a visible stubble. 'Miss?' He repeated desperately. His breath was warm, and Christine liked the smell of what she assumed was a combination of a newly eaten cinnamon bun, coffee and maybe his after shave. After she realised she must have studied his face for a few seconds, she grasped the fact that he must have studied her face as well. Suddenly, she felt quite overwhelmed having his face so close to hers. Intimidated by his closeness, she quickly looked around for cars again. To show him she was ok, she managed to move her lips to form some sort of smile.

'Oh good, you didn't hurt yourself.' His gaze changed from worried to relieved when she started laughing. He held out a hand to her, and helped her up.

Finally, Christine managed to say something.

'Thank you. I'm just embarrassed,' She laughed. 'No broken bones I think, and I didn't hurt my head.'

'I though it was only foreigners like me who feel like Bambi on these streets,' he joked. Christine made a sound that unfortunately came out like a snort.

'I forget every year how slippery these cobblestone streets can get.' She was now standing opposite him. He was a bit taller than her.

'So… you live here?' he nervously tried to start a conversation with her.

'Yes, I do. Thank you so much for helping me.' Once up on her feet, Christine quickly began to pick up her documents. He helped her and gave her the pile he had collected.

'Here ...' was all he managed to say before she interrupted him.

'So sweet of you, thank you so much. Have a lovely day!' She was so embarrassed and quickly walked away. First of all, she must have looked ridiculous, but her scream must have been too loud for the actual fall. But most of all, she was embarrassed for how long she had examined his face. It wasn't like she had been unconscious. *What an awful start to the day*, she thought. *I really hope it was just this one incident, and not a day filled with bad luck, because I really needed tonights dinner to go well..*

*

She continued to run down the street. Only when she had come to the crossing of Fredrik Stangs Gate and Bygdøy Allé did she dare to look back. *Of course he has disappeared... the opposite would have been a bit creepy I guess...* A bit disappointed, she entered the code to open the gate, and walked into the large courtyard in front of the old building. It was a large, old mansion from the beginning of the twentieth century, that was converted into an office building. A couple of cars were parked in the courtyard, but it was clear to see that they had stood there overnight, as all the windshields were completely covered in frost.

Christine thought it was strange to now work in this building, as she had always found it intimidating. Not only was the interior painted in glossy black, but it also sometimes made spooky sounds. The wooden staircase made a lot of noise when someone walked in them, but the roof often made squeaky sounds during winter.

First and foremost, however, it reminded her of the first time she had met Harald, Henrik's father. She had been quite nervous, as back then she had only known his serious face from the newspapers. Harald had actually turned out to be the nicest man she could dream of as a father-in-law, although Henrik meant he was dominating their lives. Henrik always used to say that the reason they lived so close to Harald's office was because his father could see their door from his office window, and keep track on when Henrik got up in the mornings.

In many ways, Henrik had great privileges that others could only dream of, but at the same time he was more controlled by his parents than anyone Christine knew. Since Christine now worked for Henrik's father, Harald had an even shorter leash on Henrik, as Christine naturally would give him daily updates on his son. Although she found it somewhat disloyal to Henrik to report on him so often, she felt that she had no choice but to do so since she saw Harald every day. In fact, she had felt she'd had no other choice than to accept the job Harald had offered her a few months ago either. Henrik had wanted her to accept it too, as it would put less pressure on him, and then he could continue with his dream of directing movies.

How to Avoid a Scandal

'Good morning!' Heidi said in a loud voice as Christine entered the foyer. It was still so early, and her voice was so loud, that Heidi completely startled Christine. Christine wasn't used to Heidi being there before her, which she was this morning. Heidi was a ray of sunshine, and perfect behind a reception desk. It was always funny to watch people come in because Heidi was always a little too early in her timing, so when guests and staff entered, they were usually very startled with the high volume and pitch of her greetings. Christine had even seen people drop things and almost fall because of the shock.

'My oh my, you are earlier than me today!' Christine said as she entered.

'I know, I have to go home early to get ready for tonight. I did the *getting-dressed-in-the-ladies'-room* last year, but I feel a lot better if I shower at home', Heidi gave her a wink.

'I agree. I'm going home myself, but I'm practically next door'.

'Are you excited for tonight?' Heidi asked.

'Well,' replied Christine, 'I'm ready, but I'm not really looking forward to it.' She wrinkled her nose.

'I, on the other hand, can't wait for tonight! Don't you worry, Christine, you always have me!' Heidi exclaimed enthusiastically.

Heidi was Christine's only ally at work. Among so many men, it was nice to have a female friend in the office, or just a friend in general. It was one thing to be a woman in such a competitive masculine environment, but she had even more to prove since she was practically Harald's daughter-in-law. Christine gave Heidi a brave smile and went to hang her coat in the wardrobe.

Christine dreaded the big gala that night. She had met most of the employees at the office in Oslo, but that evening, all employees, partners and clients from around the world would attend. In addition, many of Harald and his wife Wenches' personal friends would also attend, the who's who of old money, new money, and even those with no money but important official titles in Norway and across the whole of Europe. The whole thing was a great mix of important people. Christine had heard talk about there would be over four-hundred guests for dinner that night. Although she had been with Henrik since for ten years, since her teens, this would be her first year attending.

The location for the Christmas gala varied, but it was always on the first Friday in December. It was usually at one of Harald's restaurants or hotels. The party was always widely covered in national media and the press always stood at the entrance and took pictures when the guests arrived. Harald found red carpets vulgar, but it was a carpet there, and with the press coverage, it was basically the same, except you didn't stop and pose for the press. If the press got pictures when guests arrived, they would then leave. The party would go on without a camera nearby, and when the guests left in the early hours, any drunken scandals would be avoided on the front pages the next day.

The dinner would this year be at Holmenkollen Hotel. It was a grand red timber villa situated at the highest hilltop around Oslo with a great view over the city and the fjord. It was also close to the famous ski jump, and therefore was a popular place for tourists. Christine had been there for lunch once before, when her own father had two guest professors for a visit.

For the employees in Oslo, it was a tradition to gather in the office foyer for a glass of mulled wine before leaving for the gala. They usually arranged busses to take the employees to the party. The most prominent guest would be driven in nicer cars, so Christine thought it would be a good idea to hop on a bus in an attempt to avoid the media.

*

For Christine, the day passed quickly. She got through her pile of paper, she took a few calls and she ate lunch at her desk while writing a few emails. Christine hadn't dared to eat lunch with anyone else but Heidi yet, so if she knew that Heidi didn't have time for lunch, she wouldn't go down to eat. A trolley with food passed in the corridors at noon, and she usually grabbed a plate at that time.

Harald had stopped by her desk for a few minutes, but otherwise, she hadn't talked to anyone else that day. Christine was comfortable in meetings and discussing investments, but random small talk with colleagues was something she dreaded. She had had a stutter when she was a child, and she was afraid it would reappear if she was nervous. She was afraid in social situations that people would dislike her even more if they had to wait for her to finish an already boring story. So therefore, for Christine, a day with not much socialising felt like a comfortable day.

*

Eager to get lots of work done, she hadn't watched the time. She rushed home without any time to spare, even though she didn't need much time to get ready. When she left, some had already started the party a bit early in the foyer.

Outside, it was dark again, and very small snowflakes were floating around in the air, quite peacefully. The closer they came to the ground, they started swirling, like their own snowstorm. Christine realised that she hadn't been out of the office all day, so she didn't know if the sun had even appeared that day or not. It felt unreasonable that she still had to be awake for at least six more hours.

It was as cold as it had been that morning, and Christine wondered how many layers she should put on for tonight, as Holmenkollen was usually colder than in the city. The new dress was so long no one would notice if she put some layers of wool underneath her dress.

Wearing the Budget of a New Car

Christine took two steps at a time while running up the stairs. She often did that, even when she wasn't in a hurry. She found the old stairs annoyingly flat, and it was just more comfortable for her to take two steps at a time. It also went a lot quicker.

It was one of the benefits of being tall, she thought, in addition to never needing a chair to get to the highest shelves in the kitchen, nor having any problems finding your friends in a packed night club. That was about it with the advantages, though – otherwise, it was just downsides.

Christine had always been the tallest of all the girls she knew, and she had never been comfortable with her height. When she just continued to grow when everyone else stopped, she thought she was so tall that she felt she couldn't hide no matter where she was. All she wanted was to disappear, and her height made it impossible.

Slowly, over the years, she had learned to accepted her height. Of course, it had helped that the boys her age had reached puberty as well, but the insecurities she had as a teenager would always be with her. She did see that she didn't look terrible in pictures, and that being tall also meant that she never looked fat, but other than that, she did not know how beautiful other people found her.

Far from the typical Scandinavian blonde beauty, Christine therefore did not see that her Snow White look was a beautiful combination. She thought she was too tall, her body was too boyish and bony, with almost no breasts and very pale skin.

When people gave Christine a complement about her looks, it was always hard for her to believe they meant it. She always felt they were lying or just being polite. She had never felt that she was of any interest to the other gender, but on the other hand, she hadn't exactly been looking for signs. Before she had met Henrik, she did have a few crushes. Since she was very shy and had had a stutter, she had never dared to do anything about it.

Christine and Henrik had started as friends in their early teens, when she was almost a foot taller than him. They were placed next to eachother when they both were new at school. She had just moved from Bergen to Oslo with her family, and Henrik had returned from boarding school in England. They got used to doing assignments together, and became friends and confidants.

Since Christine found school pretty easy, and Henrik the contrary, she started helping him with his homework. However, Christine was always very patient, and didn't mind finding new ways to explain things to him. She never made him feel stupid, and she built his confidence.

Socially, Henrik took care of her. He was not a big guy at

first, but when he was around, no one dared to mock Christine for her stutter. He became her social crutch.

It was only when Henrik got to be the same height as her that Christine began to notice that he was looking at her a little differently than before, but she didn't understand that he was flirting. She had always thought he was handsome, and she always had a crush on him, but she thought that he looked at her only as his boring older sister, since she helped him with his homework. It was only when Henrik had tried to kiss her that she understood that he was at all interested in her that way. She still didn't quite understand why, though.

Christine unlocked the door to their massive apartment. It was on the fourth floor and fifth floor. The building was a classical apartment building, with pitched roof at the top floor. On the fourth floor was the kitchen and dining room, two guest bedrooms and their master bedroom with a large walk-in-closet, and an *en suite* with a steam room and sauna. The attic was on the fifth floor, and it had once been for drying laundry, but with some glazing put in, it also had the most splendid view over the Oslofjord. The attic was transformed into a large living room with a connecting roof terrace that overlooked the whole city and its beautiful sunsets.

When they had moved in four years ago, the whole apartment

was renovated by Harald's usual architect, and the renovation almost ended up at half of the buying price. Christine found it too big and not necessary at all, but Harald said it was a 'good investment'. Even the kitchen island cost more than the homes of some of her friends or at least a pretty nice car.

The apartment was painted white at first. Over the years, as Henrik's art collection had grown, he had ordered room by room painted a dark shade. He said white was too bright for the art, and the darker colour of the wall would bring out the colours in the artworks. Christine always felt that the apartment became bigger and scarier when it was in these dark hues. She hated coming home without knowing if Henrik was there, because she felt she had to look for him everywhere before she knew if she was alone or not. The dark colours were not to Christine's liking, but Henrik had never asked her about them beforehand.

Henrik had strong opinions, and was used to getting his own way. Christine never won if they argued. He always said after a new room was painted dark, that she could always paint the walls white again after a while, but she never did.

'Henrik? Are you home?'

There was no answer. Christine started her usual rounds of the place, room by room. When she entered the bedroom, she was not surprised that Henrik was still sleeping. She sat down beside him and started gently stroking his back.

'Henrik, you have to wake up now.'

There was no answer.

'Henrik, darling, have you picked up your jacket?'

There was still no answer.

Christine raised her voice a little to wake him up.

'Henrik, have you picked up your clothes for tonight from the cleaners?'

Henrik slowly opened just one eye.

'Hi... What?'

'Did you have a few too many last night?' Christine already knew the answer to the question. The smell in the bedroom that morning was pretty stiff, and of course she knew what it meant.

Henrik closed his eye again, and turned his head into the pillow.

'I thought you would come home straight from the airport, but you must have been home pretty late?' Christine prompted.

There was no answer from him. Christine turn on the bedside light.

'What time were you home, sweetie?'

Henrik said nothing.

'The Christmas dinner is tonight. In an hour, to be precise.' Christine said firmly.

Finally, Henrik began to move. 'Ahhh... I forgot about that.' His voice was husky, and sounded like he had been shouting a lot last night. Christine tried to stroke his head, but he pulled away.

Christine got up and walked towards to the bathroom. Her new gown was already hanging on the door, steamed and ready. Henrik had helped her pick it out in London that summer, after she had gotten some instructions from Wenche, who had booked several appointments for Christine at expensive shops around Sloane Street.

Christine was instructed that the dress had to be long, it couldn't be black. She had to send Wenche a picture for approval before deciding, and Christine was never to ask for the price. Christine had a suspicion that Wenche had already been to the shops and made a selection of the dresses she liked, and those where the ones she tried on. They were most likely already pre-approved.

She had ended up with a white strapless dress in heavy silk brocade that must have cost more than what Christine had as a budget for a new car. From the front, it looked like a column dress, cinched at the waist, but from the back there was lots of fabric that cascaded down from the top. It was simple, but still quite elaborate, and definitely made a statement. Christine thought that it made her look a bit like a tall Audrey Hepburn. If she had to go this dinner, she was glad she would wear a dress she liked, although she was hoping she wouldn't spill anything on it. *Or if that will happen, maybe it is a legitimate reason to leave?*

Everything else was laid out on the daybed; her shoes, her underwear, her stockings and her bag. Heidi had helped her with the accessories.

'Have you picked up your jacket from the dry cleaners?' She repeated her question to Henrik, she tried a calm approach. She was not angry with him, she had stopped expecting him to take responsibility years ago.

'What? No … Should I have?'

'You didn't find my note? I sent you a message, too.' Christine was not surprised at all. It looked as if nothing had happened while she had been at work.

'Why couldn't you just ask them to deliver it?'

Christine ignored the question. 'They close at six, so you'll have to run now to get it. You know we have to be in the office foyer at six, you have to go now!' Christine's voice echoed from the shower.

'Don't I have others?' Henrik yelled.

'No, you don't have several tails that fit you. You of all people cannot wear a less formal jacket.' Christine said disappointingly.

'If we had a full-time maid, she would have done this!' Henrik exclaimed.

'You are not here enough to have a full-time maid. I would rather live with you full-time than with a maid.'

Henrik followed her into the bathroom. He was now calm and opened the glass doors to the shower.

'I do have time to take a shower first, don't I?' Henrik was smiling at Christine, looking utterly charming. His cheerful grin made her heart skip a beat. He entered the shower, and immediately turned the water a bit colder, to his preference.

'Oh, Henriiiiik, you are impossible!' Christine said, a little frustrated but at the same time flirtatious. He grabbed the scrub, and handed it to her, indicating that he wanted her to scrub his back. She couldn't resist Henrik's charming smile. Seeing him happy was the most relaxing feeling, so she leaned forward to kiss him. He quickly gave her a peck. Christine sighed a bit disappointed, but knew she didn't have time for anything more anyway.

'You know I'm nervous about tonight. I need you there.'

'I thought you had Heidi there as well?'

'Heidi speaks to everyone - what do I do if she forgets me? They all know I'm with you anyway, so no one dares to speak to me unless you are there. Besides, you are much better at things like this than me!'

'Yeah, I'll be there, with my clingy girlfriend, it seems.' Henrik found some soap and started to lather.

'It's not like it's may dream job to work for you father, I am doing this for you.'

'I know, and I am very thankful for that.' Henrik said with his eyes closed.

'I have to be in the foyer before six o'clock, so they don't think I'm stuck up and don't want to mingle with them. It's very important that they see that I want to be a part of *"the office"*, not *"the family"*.

'But you are with *"the family"*. Henrik made silly punctuations in the air.

'I have to be both, and right now I have to work hard to be a part of the office. So we're taking the bus up like the rest of the office. The best way to avoid the press is to take the bus, and it will show that I am a part of that group.'

'Wouldn't it be easier for you to go incognito in a bus group if you're not with me?' Henrik asked. 'The press will definitely recognise me. Without me, though, you might be safe from them.'

Christine looked at him and raised an eyebrow.

'Okay, okay, okay! I'll hurry up. But… ' he said smiling. '… can I stay in the shower a little longer? I seriously need one. Then I'll go from a frog to a prince in seconds, I promise!'

'You do know the media call you a prince no matter what state you are in?' Christine was referring to the numerous news headlines that had reported on Henrik when he had been quite inebriated.

'That's because no matter the state, I am always charming.' Henrik grinned. He gave her a big, wet, smelly kiss on the cheek.

'But what about the pre-drinks then?' Christine looked up at him but didn't manage to stay serious, she cracked a little smile. He was just too handsome and charming to stay mad at, even when he was stinking and hung over.

'I will meet you in the foyer, maybe five minutes after you. Okay?' Henrik seemed to be very proud of his plan.

Christine was a bit sceptical, but as always, she accept his plan. She never dared to say no to him. 'Do you promise, then? Promise that you'll be there?' She looked at him with doe eyes.

'I promise.' Henrik kissed her on the forehead. 'Although, I do think mother and father only care that you come, you know you are the daughter they never had.'

Henrik always made a point of the fact that he was far from what everyone expected of him. An heir to a great fortune and son of a self-made businessman, he knew he should do his best to fill the shoes of his father.

'Stop saying that,' Christine snapped. 'The only difference is that they are not my parents, and so I can't act like you do with them. Besides, I owe our lifestyle to your parents, and I therefore feel grateful to them.'

'It is a terrible feeling that you owe someone, constantly. I never asked to be born into these expectations.'

'You don't have to feel that. You're their son, and they will always love you. I have my own parents who love me, unconditionally.'

'That's different, you're not a disappointment to your parents.'

'I'm not? My dad thinks I have sold out, working in finance.

Hwe would rather have me as a professor at a university.'

'Maybe you can have my parents then?'

'Your parents would never accept. They might "*like*" me, but, without a doubt, they "*love*" you.' Christine kissed Henrik's forehead and gave him a smile before she left the bathroom to get dressed. This was a speech she had given him over and over again, and she was starting to wonder that she would never get through.

*

'I'll see you very, very soon, then,' Christine yelled, as she was ready to leave. There was no response from the bathroom. She sighed and shrugged her shoulders and went out the door. She had her usual wool coat on, and she tried to close it even more tightly. If she had dressed for the temperature, she would have put on her massive down parka. She knew Wenche would make sure she had dressier coat for next year, as her everyday coat didn't match the dress.

There was a silver lining to wearing a huge gown, Christine thought, and that was that no one could see that she was wearing big boots and long johns under the skirt. Luckily the boots were almost the same heel height as her shoes she would put on later, but she still had to lift her skirt a bit so she wouldn't trip as she ran along the street.

Luckily, everything was frozen, so there was no need to worry about dirt. Christine carefully ran with her weight leaning forward, almost like a penguin, so she wouldn't repeat the fall from earlier.

The dress probably won't last through such a fall, she thought. Although she had her boots on, and her shoes in an old bag in her hand, her knees and thighs were so cold, she felt they were trembling.

Christine stopped at the same crossing as this morning. It was still snowing lightly. There was light snow on the ground, which swirled up in beautiful patterns each time a car passed. An old couple crossing the street to get to the bus stop. The woman was wearing an enormous fur coat, that looked pretty worn in. The woman must have shrunk, since the coat now almost reached the ground. The man she was with, held his arm around her shoulder. Maybe he wanted to warm her, or maybe they had always walked together that way. They looked like the perfect fit of puzzle pieces. Christine realised that her light had turned to *walk* without her knowing, and she tightened her belt on her wool coat, lifted her shoulders, and tied her arms in front of her to warm herself.

Champagne or Mulled Wine?

There were large torches placed all the way from the gate to the front door. They made the trees in the courtyard glow like light sculptures, as well as the old mansion. In addition, every room in the house looked lit up by candle lights in the windows. Christine had almost forgotten how harmonious the red brick building looked, so peaceful now although it was just off a busy street.

Christine had heard that the pre-drinks was usually a little less formal than the dinner afterwards. The dinner famously had a quartet at arrival, a boy choir mid dinner, and a big brass band for dancing after the dinner. Right now, though, she could hear some Christmas pop song from the foyer, not quite to Harald's classical taste.

Christine was trembling. She hoped she would find Heidi right away, but if she didn't, she had plans for how she would stall for time until Henrik arrived. She could spend some time getting a drink, she just hoped it wasn't waiters with trays, as that would take no time at all. If it was a bar, she could stand in line while looking for Heidi. She could spend some time in the cloakroom, hanging her coat, putting on her shoes, standing in line for the loo. Maybe she could let someone behind her go in front, maybe she could take her time looking at herself in the mirror, pretending to fix her hair or something. She often wondered how other girls could spend so much time in there. Sometimes she had tried to observe what other girls did in there, because for her it would always be great to be able to pass time without having to socialise. Maybe she could check her makeup like other girls do, but that would only take about a second, since she did only have a lip balm in her bag. *How on earth did other girls manage to bring so much stuff in these useless tiny clutch bags? Maybe I could practice my small talk a little with someone in the queue, someone who hopefully don't know who I am,* she thought.

Christine expected all of the female guests to be wives or girlfriends, but it wouldn't surprise her if some knew who she was from reading gossip magazines. Christine hoped that no one would recognise her from the pictures from that summer. She had been all over several magazines with Henrik in a yellow bikini, but luckily she had had sunglasses on. It had been her first time in the press, and Christine thought it was a rough start, since she didn't know she was being photographed and first time in the press she was in a bikini.

When she thought about it now, Christine realised it was pretty obvious that she as well would be photographed at some point. Henrik's life had definitely drawn a lot more attention these last years after he had started making films. The *heir-director* was his media name, as he was surrounding himself with more celebrities than before. Her incognito days with Henrik was over.

Christine took a deep breath. She checked the time, and eventually stepped close to the door and waited for the doorman to open it. The glass in the old door was covered in frost. She quivered. The cold had dug deep into her body, and her long johns hadn't helped a lot. Her legs were shaking, as well as her chin. Was it the cold or her nerves?

A wave of heat and sound hit her when the doors opened. It was boiling inside, and the main room looked full of guests. Everyone was dressed formal. It felt like she was a part of a film, set in another century. The room deserved a grand party like this, and she imagined what it must have been like when someone lived in this grand house. The music was the only thing that brought her mind back to the present. Christine gathered herself, and walked quickly into the cloakroom to the right. It was people everywhere, and the cloakroom was no exeption, so she had to wait for someone to exit to get into the area herself. She was comfortable to just stand there and wait politely, and she gently smiled at the people who left.

Christine hadn't thought about the fact that she had to get her long johns off for the pre-party, and then put them on again later. She was already feeling sweat on her lower back, and these long johns had to come off as soon as possible. She pulled up the long johns to her knees and put her shoes on. She then made her way to the bathroom to get them off properly in private.

'Is someone in there?' She asked a woman, while pointing discreetly at the door to the bathroom.

'Someone clogged it already, so we have to use the toilets by the dining room. I certainly don't recommend trying to use this one in *that* dress,' she said. Christine then realised that of course people would understand who she was based on the size of her dress, she would at least disappear in it.

'Oh, okay, thank you. The toilets there are bigger there anyway, so I might actually manage to fit in all this fabric in there. Or maybe I should have installed some sort of bedpan under here.' Christine regretted it as soon as the words came out of her mouth. She couldn't believe that she said that, that she had made small-talk about peeing before she had even had a drop of alcohol.

Obviously surprised at her comment, the woman just looked at her and then started to laugh. Christine didn't know if she laughed because she thought it was funny, or because she thought she had to. Not knowing whether people recognised her or not, made Christine very uncomfortable. She turned around quickly, and walked out of the cloakroom.

*

'Welcome, *Miss*, may I offer you a drink?' A waiter in a white shirt held a tray filled with glasses of champagne and mulled wine.

The champagne looked temptingly chilled, and Christine thought it might cool her down. Sweat was already dripping down her calves. She might take one glass to bring with her to the dining room. It would make it seem like she had been there for a while, and that she was already hanging out with friends.

'Thank you very much,' Christine said, and accepted a glass of champagne, the mulled wine would be too risky with a white dress. Christine stopped for a moment and took a big sip to cool down before she would manage herself through the crowd to get to the other toilets.

'Pardon the forwardness of my question, but how is your *bum* doing?'

Christine jumped at the sudden sound of the voice behind her. She turned around and saw two dark eyes and a friendly face smiling at her. Immediately she recognised the face, and smiled back.

'I'm not taking any chances tonight. I went for the dress that gives me room for several pillows duct-taped to my bum,' she said jokingly.

'I am delighted to see you again so soon, although maybe I shouldn't have my hopes up, since you ran off so quickly this morning,' he said seductively.

Christine gave him a shy smile, and felt a small butterfly in her stomach.

'I don't think I have ever experienced a girl run that fast away from me, was my morning breath that bad?' He said it with a hurt confidence, but Christine felt like he knew she found him attractive. Christine couldn't help but to laugh with a snort quite loudly, and she was surprised how little she managed to control it. She definitely didn't want to be observed flirting with a man at her *in-laws* party.

He gave her no time to reply, and he rambled on. '… but, I am very pleased to see you and your bum in good condition this evening, not that I have looked. I just assumed since you are standing up.' He stretched out his hand to introduce himself, and she noticed that it had a small tremble. 'I'm Charlie Lawson, from the London office. It's a pleasure to meet you, Miss…?'

She noticed that her palms were sweaty, so she reached out her hand with a bit of embarrassment. Her forehead would soon break out in sweat, and she could also feel that a drop of sweat run down from the back of her knee, where her pulled up long johns made the dress unbearably warm. 'Løvness, but call me Christine. I started this September at the Oslo office.'

'Christine, there you are! I've been looking everywhere for you!' Heidi was shouting from the middle of the stairs. 'I'm coming down to you now, stay where you are!'

Christine looked back at Charlie. He smiled at her, his gaze locked on her.

'Loveness?'

'Yes, that is correct, or almost at least. It's pronounced with a more open *"o"* sound than in the word *"love"*. Kind of like the *"ur"* sound in *"bird"*.'

'That's a *"luuvely"* name. So ... you know everyone here then, *Miss Loveness*?' Charlie clearly had no intention of trying to pronounce her name correctly. He looked around the room, and at her again.

'Not exactly ...' she said.

Heidi was a few yards away, and when she was in reach, she threw herself around Christine's neck. 'Hiiiiiiii! Jeesus, you are boiling, is that dress made of silk and cashmere or something?' Heidi said as she pulled away. Christine didn't manage to reply, and stood there while her blushing went from a glow to dark red. 'You didn't go for the mulled wine? Clever choice! I thought I was safe since I am wearing black, but after I had already had two, I learned that there was extra vodka in it this year, in addition to the red wine. Do they *want* us to make fools out of ourselves?' Heidi exclaimed like a stand-up comedian. Christine and Charlie both laughed. Heidi's unique way of making Christine feel comfortable, had started to kick in.

'Where's Henrik by the way?' Heidi stepped back and continued talking: 'You look *amazing*! Oh my God, I know your figure looks good in *everything*, but that dress makes you look like Hollywood royalty!' Heidi suddenly looked at Charlie for an agreeing confirmation.

'I agree,' Charlie added nervously. 'I didn't get to that yet, but it was the first thing I thought too….' All of a sudden, Charlie was pushed by another guest, and started speaking to him. Heidi pulled Christine aside.

'Who is that *gorgeous* guy you were speaking to? And why didn't you introduce me?' Heidi bombarded Christine with questions, and it wasn't easy for Christine to get a word in.

'Calm down a bit, will you? His name is Charlie Lawson. More, I do not know. Please, *Heidi*, breathe.'

Christine turned to face Charlie again, ready to introduce them to each other, but he was now preoccupied speaking to another guest.

'I think I'll hook up with Charlie tonight, he looks very kissable,' Heidi whispered, giving Christine a naughty smile. Christine laughed and shook her head.

'*What?*' Heidi replied offendedly. 'It's not easy being single. I have to rely on occasions like these, when I look my very best, to get some action. You can have Henrik whenever you want …'

If he's home, Christine thought to herself.

'Unless *you* want Charlie…' Heidi continued. 'I noticed you were blushing, when you spoke to him. I have never seen you like that around a guy. It's about time you did something naughty in your life.' Heidi grabbed a glass of champagne from a tray that passed them.

'Do I have to remind you of the reason why *I* am here tonight?' Christine looked at Heidi as if she had suggested a preposterous idea.

'Where is he anyway?' Heidi asked as she looked around the room.

*

'We can't wait any longer now. I'm freezing to death, and I just want to go inside the bus!' Heidi exclaimed as they stood by the last bus in the courtyard.

Henrik was not there yet, nor did he answer his phone. Christine was not surprised, as Henrik was always late, if he would show up. She had hoped Henrik had understood how important it was to her that he was by her side tonight.

'I know, I know … I will try him one more time,' Christine took up her phone once again.

'Why aren't you cold?' Heidi looked at her. Christine just lifted her skirt so Heidi could see her long johns.

'*Ah*, that explained why you were sweating like a pig when we spoke to the cute guy. I thought you had *the hots* for him," Heidi seemed quite proud of her word pun. Christine hung up her phone, since there was no answer from Henrik.

'I don't have the *hots* for Charlie, but this guy called John who is quite long is giving me a *warm feeling..*' Christine said ironically as Heidi burst out laughing.

'I'll have to go by myself then,' Christine thought disappointingly, and she looked towards the entrance of the bus.

'Stop complaining. You're not by yourself, you have *me*!'

Heidi gave her a big, comforting smile.

But it wasn't the same, as she could not just stand next to Heidi and listen, like she would with Henrik. Heidi always spoke to everyone, and she had no idea what it was like to be shy. She had always loved attention and couldn't get enough.

Heidi's almost-estranged father had once been a quite famous international football player, and she had used his status as much as she possibly could. She loved the attention she got from being a minor celebrity. She was just famous enough to get an invitation to all parties worth going to, but ultimately, she had no interest in making a living out of being a celebrity.

Everyone loved to hang out with Heidi, and Christine often thought that people must wonder why Heidi bothered to drag Christine along. They were such an unlikely match. Christine was tall, dark, serious and shy, and Heidi was tiny, blonde, fun loving, and outgoing. They had been best friends since they were sixteen. Christine relaxed around Heidi, and her humour came out around Heidi, which made her Heidi's favourite sidekick.

They had lived together while they had both studied in Bergen, but while Christine had graduated with a top degree from business school, and spent most nights studying, Heidi hadn't even finished her degree of random subjects, mainly because of too many social event she simply couldn't miss.

While Christine had just started doing investments for Harald, Harald had offered Heidi a job as a receptionist a couple of years ago. Heidi was not known for being very effective nor organised, but she was a great hostess, and great with people, and Harald always wanted his guests to enter and leave his office with a smile. When Heidi welcomed guests in the foyer, you could hear her all throughout the building. Her smile was disarming, and she had no ambition of having any other job within the firm.

*

The bus was struggling up hill to Holmenkollen, and it felt like it was moving slower after each turn. It was still slightly snowing, but Christine was hoping they would get above the clouds, and the view from the hotel would be spectacular as it could be.

'I'm actually a bit happy that Henrik is late. I get to sit next to you on the bus, and you can stand with me before we're seated,' Heidi whispered to Christine.

'What do you mean? You have loads of friends at the office,' Christine looked at her questionably.

'That's true, but it seems like everyone is different when they have their wives with them. They don't want to show their wife that they are besties with the blonde, not-so-clever receptionist.'

It hadn't crossed Christine's mind that even in some situations, even Heidi felt a bit uncomfortable. 'Don't you have a pretty good overview of who's single and who's not?' Christine tried to cheer her up a bit.

'That's true,' Heidi agreed. "But it's actually not that many of them, and they all manage to find *someone* to bring along tonight, as if they'll get a higher bonus or something if they show they're providers.'

'That actually might be the reason,' Christine wondered. Heidi was smarter than what you would expect, at times.

'I wish there was some secret sign if people had a fake girlfriend with them. Sort of like a traffic party, very discrete of course, it would be so useful!' Heidi laughed and continued: 'At least the people from the London office should be fun. None of them brought any better-halves!'

Christine laughed: 'I am glad I'm your friend, otherwise I would be pretty threatened with you around Henrik, but luckily, he's never at the office!'

'Why do they call it a 'better-half' anyway? It's so ironic, aren't we pretty great by ourselves? I don't find your half better than you.'

'Speaking of …' Christine could feel her phone vibrating. Just when she had forgotten all about Henrik, he called. They were already half-way there.

'Where are you?' Christine didn't have the patience to say hello first.

'Hey, sorry, I had forgotten the cuff links, so had run home again. I'm sorry I didn't make it before the buses left, but I *am* on my way. Dad's car is picking me up now. He just dropped mum and dad off.'

'Working hard on improving your public image, I see…' she hissed through her teeth.

'Don't worry, a bus drive wouldn't change anything,' Henrik replied.

Forty Going on Sixty

The hotel was perfectly lit like a magical winter wonderland. The cold had created a layer of frost on absolutely everything, and trees, fences, lamps, rails were sparkling like crystals. The sky wasn't crystal clear, there was still some layer of fog, but the stars were shining a lot brighter through the clouds since they where away from the city lights. The fjord was outlined by the warm lights from the houses all along the shore, safe from the harsh brightness of the city.

The snow made a crusty sound underfoot, the sound only those who have experienced a really cold winter would know about.

As Christine stepped off of the bus, she spotted Harald and Wenche by the entrance. They were standing at the top of the stairs and greeted all of the guests at the door. Christine was caught by surprise when she saw that the media were already surrounding the door, and she felt her nerves getting to her.

'Give me your bag and scarf. Quick!' Heidi was thinking a lot faster than Christine.

'Let your coat slip look like you're in a fashion advert. Next year you're not wearing a coat at all.'

'All I know is that it is a coat, but how would it hang in and advert?' Christine was stressed, and didn't know what to do.

'Take it off, and just give it to me then, and pull up you long gloves.'

Christine followed Heidi's instructions in a hurry while freezing to death, hiding behind some guests in front of her so the photographers wouldn't see her wardrobe change. As they approached the entrance, the flashes started. The photographers had done their homework, and recognised her.

Heidi was no longer by her side, and Christine took a quick look back for her. Heidi had stopped a few meters behind her and was holding her scarf and bag. It was all too big for her petite frame, and she looked like a pack mule. Heidi had ruined her own photograph so that Christine would look great. She smiled at Christine, and motioned that Christine should smile too.

As Christine approached her almost parents-in-law, she focused on walking gracefully. Wenche opened her arms towards her and gave her a kiss on both cheeks.

'Where on earth is Henrik?' Wenche whispered to Christine thought her teeth, smiling the whole time.

'He's on his way, we'll just say that he is delayed or something. It'll just sound like he missed his flight,' Christine said in a low voice, so that the photographers wouldn't hear her.

'Well, you're here at least,' Harald said as he gave her a hug.

As Christine was about to walk inside, Harald signalled to Heidi that he would take Christine's coat, so the photographers would get a great shot of Heidi as well. Harald also pushed Christine to give the press a few more images. She felt exposed, but knew she had to pretend, so she turned her head and smiled at the photographers.

*

Once she was inside, Christine quickly walked around the corner. She leaned her head against the wall and took a deep breath. She didn't care if the other guests saw her. Her heart was still jumping.

All of a sudden, Heidi was next to her. 'Sweetheart! You were A-M-A-Z-I-N-G. I am so proud of you! That pose, with your head turned, was fantastic! I know how hard that was for you. Although you *definitely* have the looks for this life, I am not sure you have the confidence.' Heidi was all smiles and proud as a mama bear. Christine smiled at her. It was so comforting having her there.

'I can't believe this is your life, Christine. Harald and Wenche are so sweet, you're so lucky!' Heidi obviously regretted saying that as she said it, since she quickly added: '…with your in-laws, I mean.'"

Christine knew that Heidi was a bit envious of her life sometimes, mostly all the holidays and the unlimited spending. They both knew that Heidi would have been a lot more comfortable with all the attention than Christine.

'They are wonderful,' Christine conceded, 'but you know, I

see them more than Henrik lately.'

Heidi knew that living with Henrik was not as easy as it looked like from the outside, so she didn't argue. She quickly changed the subject to the stylish venue as they walked into the reception area. They both grabbed a glass of champagne.

'By the way, have you talked to anyone from London besides the cutie you met in the foyer?' Heidi asked.

'No, I haven't,' replied Christine. 'Besides, I didn't really talk to him properly, either.'

'I've heard rumours that Harald is going to announce his new right-hand man in London tonight,' Heidi began. 'Apparently he's this not-*too*-old hotshot who was also wanted for this billion-dollar Silicon Valley tech company.'

'Oh, which one?' Christine was curious, as maybe this was worth knowing for future investments.

Heidi rolled her eyes at Christine. 'How am *I* supposed to know?' She said as she was scouting the room for the subject.

'Well, every other gossip seem to stick, out of the hundreds of names you remember, maybe a company name would stick as well,' Christine mumbled as she took a sip.

'Only what is useful sticks..' She said ironically. 'Anyway, I think I am going to talk to him, this new guy, after I find out who he is. He might be a potential casual boyfriend. It can be pretty practical to have a casual boyfriend in London." Heidi seemed pretty confident that this man was worth knowing.

"Do you know anything about him besides that he's the new head of the London office?' Christine was quite sceptical about Heidi's plan. She took a sip from her glass and started to look around the room as well.

'I know enough to consider him at least,' Heidi smiled. 'I know that he is closer to our age than our parents at least. It would be fun to date a hot shot for a while, and of course, Henrik is taken.'

'You should date someone rich or at least someone more famous than yourself so that you can see that it's not as glamorous as you think. Maybe you'll start to appreciate a more ordinary guy after afterwards,' Christine said it with a sadness to her voice.

"'I guess that is true - I'll probably never settle with someone until I know that I'm not missing anything,' Heidi agreed. 'Which brings us back to this .. Harald must pay this new London guy REALLY well, so I am certain he will be my next date. Who could he be?' Heidi had turned around to scouting another part of the room.

'You should probably look for someone who's about forty, but looks like he's had enough *foie gras* and expensive red wine that he looks like he is pushing sixty. Oh, and let's not to forget the great glow of a meeting room complexion… I think you should rather go for Charlie, the guy we barely talked to in the foyer. He's very handsome,' Christine regretted it as soon as she said it. Why would she set up Heidi with the guy she had felt a spark with? Wouldn't it be better to have him disappear than to have him involved in Heidi life?

'He was super cute, I'll have him as a backup. In case this new guy is appalling or has his wife with him. I'm not dating a married one every again.' Heidi was starting to walk towards the seating plan.

'Do you think the office ink is a better idea?' Christine left her glass on a small table, although she had barely had a sip or two of it. She thought she should be quite careful, considering all eyes would be on her tonight.

'I know. It's all doomed before anything has started, really,' Heidi said. 'I know it will lead absolutely nowhere, which is the point, It's at least entertaining until someone I really like comes along. At least one of us has some hilarious dating stories to make us laugh when we're ninety. You can't say I don't have a few of those…'

Christine laughed, but knew it was all a defence mechanism from Heidi. She had her heart broken when they were nineteen, and had just had silly flings since then, where she had always had the upper hand.

They both laughed as Heidi retold a story where she had been on a date with a guy who turned out to be a gospel composer as they walked towards the dining rooms.

This hotel was not ideal for this type of event, as there was not one great room but several in a row. It was less intimidating, but it was not easy getting an overview of who was there and what was happening in other rooms. The painted timber walls were in different dark colours, dark red, dark green, and charcoal, and all rooms had a fireplace and big chandeliers. It was a cosy and intimate atmosphere.

Heidi and Christine found the seating plan, and as Christine expected, they were placed rather far apart. Christine was placed in the most formal main room, at the biggest table. Heidi seemed almost banished to a room far away, along with other insignificant and easily replaceable employees. Typically, Heidi was not upset about being unimportant, she was just annoyed that her flirting plans seemed harder to follow through.

'Ah, of course, I'll be far away from the new guy in London with that seating. I thought I might be bumped up this year, as Harald always brags about how good I am at small talk. You have to be on the lookout for me, and then you can introduce me!'

'You never let anything stop you, and you always charm everyone, so I'm sure the rumours of this gorgeous and funny girl in a room far away will reach him.'

'I know I laugh loudly, but I really hope I don't laugh that loud..' Heidi jested.

Christine sometimes wished she had Heidi's ease with people, and her ability to charm and entertain a whole room without the intention. Heidi just had fun wherever she was. Christine looked at the chart. She found her name at the same table as Harald and Henrik. Her heart jumped when she also noticed Charlie's name at the same table, but she didn't say anything about it to Heidi.

'I, on the other hand, have been less fortunate with my dining partner. I got Alex Weeum-Hansen.'

Christine sighed.

'Oh,' Heidi agreed. 'You'll survive. You've managed him for what, ten years? You'll be fine. Just don't let him get to you. Look on the bright side, you don't care what he thinks about you.' Heidi always managed to see things in a positive way.

Christine was not looking forward to being next to Alex. Harald probably thought she would find it comforting, since he had been in their class at school and had also attended business school with Christine.

The thing was, Christine had always found Alex a bit of a bully. He was Henrik's neighbour from childhood, and they had practically grown up together, but they had always fought a lot. Alex had been the opposite of Henrik in so many ways. He had always been mean. He was not too bad at sports but excelled at school. He had always treated Henrik badly, but he was so polite and obsequious toward all adults.

He had never been particularly nice to Christine either, and he was always quite condescending. At business school, Christine had found his behaviour towards others arrogant, and she thought he was quite the pig, especially if he had downed a glass or two.

Alex had come from a quite well-off family, but they had nowhere near the fortune that Henrik would one day inherit. Alex had, unlike Henrik, an extreme appetite for money, and did not hide it. He wanted so badly to succeed at his businesses, since his parent's money could not nearly cover the certain lifestyle he wanted. Alex had therefore always been jealous of Henrik, not just for his looks and popularity, but mostly for the fact that Henrik's would one day inherit a great fortune.

The worst part was how Alex acted more flirtatious towards her when Henrik was around, and to Christine it was quite obvious that he did that to annoy Henrik.

Christine's seat was along one of the sides of a very long and narrow table, with Harald sat at the centre. Surrounding her was all of Scandinavia's richest people. Henrik was placed a couple of seats from her on the same side of the table, so she could not make eye contact with him. She would maybe get in contact with him behind Alex and his dining partner's backs. But that didn't matter now, because he had not shown up yet.

Christine greeted Alex politely, who was smug as always.

'Wasn't I the luckiest man tonight, getting you by my side? I told Harald that you have grown up pretty nicely since your nose-was-bigger-than-your-face days as a teenager.'

'Thanks…I guess,' Christine said, not knowing whether it was a compliment on her looks tonight, or a comment on how hopeless her looks where when they were younger.

'When you got it fixed, why didn't you get a discount for those sad things someone might all boobs as well?' Alex had obviously had a few too many already.

Christine had no idea what to answer. She didn't know where to start, she had neither had a nose-job, nor did she have any interest of discussing her breasts. She looked around the table, to see if anyone overheard what Alex just said. The seat next to her was still empty, and she noticed an English name on table card. She looked at the other side of the table and saw Charlie standing behind a chair. He was a couple of seats closer to Harald than what she was. *Could it be him?* she thought. *The new head of London could definitely have that seat.* Charlie looked very young to get that position, but Christine knew that Harald wouldn't have given that seat to someone that wasn't very important, either within the organisation or a collaborator. He was seated in close proximity to both Harald and Wenche, and had the wife of Harald's best friend next to him. Charlie tried to polity greet the other guest, as they arrived at the table, but he didn't engage in any particular small talk with other guest. He was fidgeting with his cufflinks, when suddenly he caught her looking at him. He gave her a shy smile. Christine was so startled that instead of giving a friendly smile back at him, she quickly looked away. *Oh no*, she thought. *Now he thinks I am interested in him.* The man seated next to her also arrived, and Christine barely managed to greet to him before Harald rang a small bell. As the bell rang, Christine could see Henrik enter the room, trying to find his way to his seat. He was so comfortable being late. It was obvious that he didn't feel embarrassed or rushed at all, rather the contrary, he said hello to people and gave them hugs and kisses, as though he was stealing his father's thunder. He looked amazingly handsome. His blonde curls were slicked back, and his skin looked like he had just returned from holiday, which he always was, in a way. His white teeth gave him the smile of a superstar actor. Everyone who met him was astonished by his good looks. Christine couldn't resist smiling when she saw Henrik. She couldn't believe he was her boyfriend. As Henrik made quite the entrance, Harald started his speech. He welcomed and thanked his partners and employees and summed up what they had achieved that year. From the corner of her eye, Christine sensed that Charlie was staring at her during the speech. She must have imagined it, but to be sure, she quickly looked in his direction. She caught herself blushing when their eyes met. He wasn't embarrassed that she had caught him, and gave her a friendly nod. He kept his gaze on her; he was clearly not embarrassed to be caught looking at her at all. *Oh, won't you be surprised when you see who I am here with … Christine* thought to herself.

Harald's speech went on. 'Yes, you all know that I have been searching for a new chief for the London office, and of course I wanted the very best candidates I could possibly find. First of all, he knows how to lead, as he has had a great career already, despite his young age. He was already a name in the industry before the age of 27, and has continued to rise since then. I am very lucky that he agreed to come to us. I am very proud to introduce you to Charlie Lawson! Get up here, Charlie!' Harald exclaimed.

The whole room looked at Charlie, but Christine resisted. He put his napkin on the table, and pulled his chair back. On his way to Harald, he gave Christine a grin while adjusting his cufflinks again. Christine looked away right before their eyes met, and thought to herself: *Oh, you think that with that position I will fall at your feet, don't you? Just wait until you find out who I am.*

Charlie said some polite words to Harald before he started his speech. He took up a small note. Christine noticed his hand was shivering when he struggled to find a word. He said that he was looking forward to getting started, and that he felt humble representing such a great family and business. He finished off by saying something about looking forward to spending some time in Oslo, which he found quite exotic, and getting to know everyone at the Oslo office as well. As he finished off, Christine made sure their eyes did not meet, although she knew he was looking in her direction.

Harald continued to speak after Charlie. 'I also have a second introduction I want to make. As you know, my son has transformed his talent for making ski films to writing and directing films for the silver screen. My lovely wife, Wenche, and I are very excited and proud of him, but we are very much wondering where that interest actually came from, as none of us have that strong artistic side. Since he is currently chasing fame and, I almost said *"fortune"*...' Harald started to laugh, and the guest started to laugh politely as well.

'Well, chasing fame, at least, we are very happy that he managed to come all the way from Los Angeles just for tonight. I guess we can all forgive him for being a little late, and I am sure he will make it up to us and party until his plane leaves tomorrow. Henrik, will you get up here?'

Harald looked proudly at Henrik, overacting a bit, Christine thought. He wasn't proud like that in private. Henrik jumped up cheerfully, his curls bouncing around like a surfer running towards the sea.

'As you all know, Henrik will at some point take over the majority of the shares, but with his busy schedule in the film industry, Wenche and I are in the meantime very happy that his girlfriend, I would say almost wife, Christine, who we consider our very own daughter, has stepped into the family business. We are very pleased that someone of that calibre, who actually has a genuine interest, has agreed to learn the ropes at my office. With a splendid former career as a financial analyst, with a work ethic that really impresses me, and let us not forget that she is clever and charming. Let me introduce you to our wonderful Christine!'

Christine felt that Harald was shouting at her. She wanted to disappear, but she realised she had to go up to Harald and Henrik now. As she got up, she couldn't help herself but to take a quick look at Charlie to see his expression when he realised who she was. She didn't know whether it was intentional or not, but Charlie avoided her, and was now whispering something to the lady next to him. *This was my secret*, Christine thought. *I'm practically your boss' daughter-in-law.* Henrik said something that made the whole party laugh, but Christine didn't catch the joke as she walked towards them. As she greeted Harald, her pulse was intense. Out of the corner of her eye, she felt that Charlie was watching her again. When she was then ready to give Henrik a kiss, he held out his hand for her to grab. After she accepted it, he then twirled her around like they were Fred Astaire and Ginger Rogers, and he then dipped her very low, and kissed her on the mouth when her head was a few feet above the floor. It probably looked amazing, but it was not comfortable at all, and Christine was afraid that he would let her slip. When she got up, Henrik gave her another kiss. He smiled at her, and she couldn't help but smile either, although she was furiously mad because of that performance which could have gone terribly wrong. Henrik was all about having fun, and couldn't fathom how traumatic that all would have been for shy Christine.

    Henrik started to speak to the crowd about her: 'My leading

lady, my boss, my rock, my love. She is a lot more suited to this than me; she is analytical, decisive, calm, sensible and a hell of a lot smarter than I am. My father is so lucky to have her replace me, and the rest of you are so lucky to have her in the business rather than me.' Christine was moved by his words, and she could feel her eyes filling up with tears. Henrik didn't express his emotions for her that often. She squeezed his hand quite hard. Luckily she didn't have to say anything. Both Henrik and Harald knew her so well that they didn't force her to do that. After those supportive words, Christine was all right for the rest of the night. Alex was mostly preoccupied with talking about stock markets with someone across the table, and the guest on Christine's other side was a funny old English man, and Christine enjoyed his company.

*

Henrik checked in at her a few times during dinner, to make sure Alex didn't offend her too much. He came up to her in between courses, and he acted exactly how she had hoped for that night. The fact that he had been away for two months was almost forgotten, and Christine felt that the rest of the night was almost magical, as if it was a dream, and she had the dream boyfriend.

*

On their way home, Christine felt like she was flowing on air.

Henrik had been great, but she couldn't get Charlie completely of her head. She had always known that others were envious of her relationship with Henrik, but tonight, she had felt that someone was maybe envious of Henrik for dating *her*. It was a strange feeling, she felt guilty for maybe leading someone on a bit, when she really wasn't interested, but it also felt nice that someone could be interested in her without knowing who she was dating. *Or maybe I am just imagining the whole thing*, she thought.

The 'Not So Social' Social Event

'Will I see you tonight, Christine?' Harald was standing in the door to Christine's office.

'Yes, you certainly will. It was very nice of Skogstad to invite me and not Henrik, I really didn't expect that.'

'Skogstad knows that you're the one representing the both of you. It has become a nice tradition, this concert,' Harald began: 'It's a way for Skogstad to wish all his employers and collaborators a "Merry Christmas". You don't have to enjoy it, it's just important that you show up, say hello or just nod to all the people that you recognise, sit there and listen, then nod to people on your way out, then go home.'

Christine was trying to hide her amusement. 'The choir singing is pretty nice as well, isn't it?'

'Yes, of course,' Harald mumbled. 'I have a meeting at four, so the I will be driven there directly. Let me know if you want the car to pick you up as well.'

'Thanks, but I think I'm okay. I need the walk, and some fresh air,' Christine said. She would rather sneak in late, nod to everyone she recognised from a bench in the back. It was a social work gathering that didn't require talking at all, but she knew Harald would take every opportunity to small talk with everyone on their way in, and get a seat so everyone could see he was present.

*

The church lay on a hill, in the middle of the city. The cobblestone walkway to the top was covered in snow. It was already dark when Christine got there, and she was quite cold from the walk over, so she accepted a glass of mulled wine to bring inside. The red brick church was candlelit, and almost completely full when she entered. Her plan to arrive a bit late worked perfectly. She saw several familiar faces, and to the people that looked her way, she waved and said 'Merry Christmas'. So many were with a date, and some had even brought their whole family with them. Christine felt joy and relaxed when she saw men in suits that were usually very serious, become different people with their children around, it was as if what they did during the day, didn't really matter, family and your loved ones was all that mattered in the world.

During the concert, Christine felt goosebumps on her neck, She hadn't felt so much in years, like the concert was knocking on the wall she hid behind. She wasn't religious at all, but she did have good memories of that choir playing from her childhood, especially on Christmas Eve, when her dad put a record of them on. All the memories she had as a child, she wanted to create them herself, when her parents would no longer be there. Although Henrik usually found all classical music boring, she knew he would be as moved as she was if he had been there. Only a heart of stone could not have been moved by the young boy singing as a solo.

As she sat there, she felt tears in her eyes, but managed to remove them, pretending to have something in her eye, right before they rolled down her cheek. She was in a church filled with families and love, and she felt so incredibly lonely. It was as if she hadn't realised that the emptiness she had been feeling for quite a while was loneliness. She took her phone out of her pocket. Henrik still hadn't replied to her last text. She started typing.

I miss you. I don't want to be apart as often as we are.

She pressed send, closed her eyes, and wished that Henrik was by her side. She wished he was with her not just for the concert, but every day.

*

Since Christine had found a seat at the back of the church, it didn't take her too long to get outside when the concert was over. It would take forever to wait for Harald, so she decided to be a bit rude and leave.   As Christine stepped down the last step of the stairs outside, all of a sudden Charlie was in front of her. She hadn't noticed him inside. His ears were red already, and his wool peacoat looked a bit too thin for the Oslo weather.

'Hi! So nice to run into you again,' he said, while he gave Christine a kiss on each cheek.

'Likewise,' she replied, forgetting that English gave two kisses. He went on as if the awkward situation hadn't happened:

'What an amazing concert, I had goosebumps almost the whole time.'

'Yes, it really gets you in the Christmas spirit, doesn't it?' Christine replied.

'I was wondering if you and Henrik would like to join me for a cup of coffee, or maybe an Irish one?'

'Henrik is not with me, actually. He left Saturday morning, because he had to continue filming,' Christine was sure that he knew that already, as Harald must have mentioned it to him.

'Oh, how about just you, then? The night is still young,' he asked with a big grin.

'Mind if I take a rain-check? I'm rather tired.'

'Anytime. Which way are you going? It is quite dark, and you know dark means dangerous.'

'Dangerous?' Christine laughed. Dangerous was not the word she would use to describe the neighbourhood they were in.

'When I say dangerous, I do mean dangerous as in slippery.' They looked at each other and laughed.

'I'm heading towards the office, I live close by.' Christine said laughingly.

'As do I.' Charlie said hastily.

*

'I hope you had a nice weekend in Oslo?' Christine started the conversation as they walked along the street.

'Yes, I did indeed,' Charlie began: 'So many people out in

bars everywhere. I's such a contrast, that it is so cold and quiet outside, and so packed with people inside, wether it is a restaurant or a bar.'

'I'm glad you enjoyed Oslo in December.'

'I really like it here, people are very friendly or at least our colleagues in the Oslo office are really nice, but I guess you know that already.'

Christine hesitated. 'I don't know that many people at the office yet. They all seem a bit afraid of me, because of Henrik, and it doesn't help that I am quite shy, which probably is perceived as arrogance.'

'I can see why they are intimidated by you, but you don't seem too shy with me?' He looked at her flirtatiously.

'Well, that's because the first time I met you, I was lying flat out in the street. Can't get any worse than that.' Christine joked.

He laughed. 'I am glad it a least made you relax.'

'You didn't know who I was at the time either.'

'I would never imagine you as Henrik's girlfriend.'

Christine quickly looked at the ground, not knowing what to say or do. She knew she wasn't the stunning beauty that Henrik obviously could be with, but he didn't have to point out the obvious.

'I mean, you were working at the cafe at a very early hour. I don't mean to insult Henrik by saying that I didn't expect his girlfriend to be up early or having a proper job.'

'Nice save', Christine jested. 'So you know Henrik quite well?'

'Well, I know of him. I was actually at school with Henrik. I don't think he remembers me. I was two years above him, but I remember him quite well. He was a cool kid, hung out with older boys. I, on the other hand, was a nobody.'

'Henrik has always said that he had a horrible time. Is that what all of you privileged kids do, complain about how terrible boarding school is?'

'I guess that came off as rather spoiled. I was very fortunate to go there. I was accepted because my dad taught there. He is a professor in history.'

'So is mine!'

'Really? Then you know the income doesn't necessarily signify a great fortune.'

'Did you ever feel like you belonged there?'

'Of course I felt out of place. But then you realise that there is good and bad people everywhere, with or without money. You can't lose your self-worth because someone acts more important than you.'

'Hm.' Christine said. *Do I come off as submissive of Henrik's wealth? Would we be a better fit, if we were more equal financially?*

'Do you ever get jealous of him? Of his wealth I mean.' Charlie looked at her.

'Interesting you put it that way. Most people think I am very lucky to be with Henrik, but I guess you understand it's not my money at all. Sometimes I think maybe he would be more content, without having this need of being something great on his own.'

'Ah, the typical paradox of being an heir to a fortune.' Charlie said it as if it was a common problem. 'Can't be easy to live with that. Have you known him for a long time?'

Christine was getting colder and folded her hands in front of her as she walked.

'We sort of grew up together. I got to know him when he returned home to Oslo at fifteen or something, then we got together at sixteen, when he finally reached my height. I couldn't believe how lucky I was, that he wanted to be with me.'

'I think Henrik is pretty lucky. I have heard a thing or two about you from Harald, you see.'

'Well, thank you for your flattery. Since you are in some ways my boss, I should take that as a compliment, but we both know that Henrik is like a star, everyone turns around whenever he walks into a room.'

'It's that attitude I remember him by. I was so envious of that attitude.'

'So you are what they call a late bloomer then?'

Charlie stopped and looked at Christine. 'Whatever do you mean?'

'Didn't you just tell me you were a geek at school? You must have girls drooling over you now, right Charlie?' Christine had a humous tone in her voice, and tried to meet his eyes.

Charlie was blushing and avoided the question. He looked towards the building opposite.

'I never got an answer from you about that drink, did I? How about a cup of hot chocolate? I am definitely having one, so do you mind waiting for a minute?'

They were outside of the cafe already. Christine didn't know how to tell Charlie that she was only twenty meters from her door. Charlie went inside, and Christine thought it was a bit strange to follow him inside, since he had said he'd just wanted her to wait. Instead, she went across the street, and looked at the magazine covers in the window of the corner shop. She heard the bell ring again and looked across the street and smiled at Charlie. He had a cup in each hand.

'If you don't want it, I will drink them both. However, I don't need the calories, so please spare me an extra run after Christmas.'

Christine grabbed a cup: 'I couldn't resist the temptation. You're not fat, though.'"

'I am not so sure about that.' Charlie pulled his chin down and made an extremely bad double-chin. Christine burst out laughing.

Quickly, they reached the front door of Christine's house.

'This is me.' Christine said.

'Oh, that's a very short walk to work. You can walk in your pyjama.'

'Yeah, I think that was the intention from Harald, but it's not really helping Henrik to spend more time there, through.' She paused and grinned: 'Thanks for the walk and the hot chocolate.'

'My pleasure,' Charlie said. He was still right in front of the door, and seemed in no rush to leave. Christine was wondering if he was lingering for an invitation to come inside.

'I guess I'll see you around?' Christine said and opened the door.

'Yes, definitely,' he said and nodded. Christine closed the door behind her and started walking up the stairs.

*

She drank the last sip and left the empty cup on the round table in the hallway. On the table was a note from the cleaning lady, wishing them a merry Christmas. She had probably found Christine's Christmas card and gift that she had put out that morning.

Once she was in her night gown, Christine sat down in the lounge chair that overlooked the backyard. She started to write a "thank you text" to the cleaning lady. She then tried to call Henrik. She lied down at the bed, and decided to lie in the middle. She fell asleep almost instantly.

The Second Year

Behind the Green Door

'This is good, you can just let me off right here. I'll walk the rest, it is so tricky to turn in there.'

'Are you sure, Miss?' The taxi driver said as he stopped.

'Yes, absolutely. Thank you!'

Christine got out of the black cab with her little carry-on suitcase and dress bag. The sky had cleared up, and the sunlight was much warmer than back home. She loved the London light in the winter, like a Turner painting. The cobblestones were shining, it looked like it had just been raining.

Christine walked along the small mew, her carry-on making an awfully loud sound as it rolled along on the cobbled street. All the small houses were so well taken care of, with newly painted doors, pottery with beautiful flowers, and polished doorknobs. Christine was in front of the green door she had stood in front of so many times before in Stanhope Mews. As she had done every time before, she paused, not knowing what to expect. She rang the bell, waited a few seconds, and tried to twist the doorknob. It was open. Henrik stood in the middle of the room and smiled: 'Hi sweetheart!'

'Henrik!'

Christine almost shouted and threw her arms around his neck. He squeezed her properly and lifted her off the floor.

'Be careful with my hair,' she warned him. 'It's ready for tonight. I stopped by the hairdresser on my way here.'

He was warm, and wearing a t-shirt and the chunky cashmere trousers he always wore hanging around the house. He looked like a slob, but Christine knew that they were the most expensive sweatpants and t-shirt he could find. His skin felt warm and smelled like he hadn't showered in a while. She used to love that smell. Or was it really that same smell? Still hugging, she looked over Henrik's shoulder. The kitchen was messy, and she noticed the wine glasses at once. There were two used wineglasses on the table. Christine took off her scarf and coat and lay them over her carry-on which she had left by the door.

'Did you have guests last night?' she asked in a nice voice, trying to not sound suspicious.

'You're not going to kiss me first?' He smiled lovingly at her with his beautiful white teeth. She kissed him with closed lips and made a sweet sound.

'Since you haven't showered, and the kitchen was quite messy, I assume you had a nice evening last night, and I was just wondering how it was.' Christine tried to make it less of an interrogation, and more like a conversation.

'Yeah, a couple of people from the crew stopped by before we went out to a bar in Shoreditch,' Henrik lifted his arm and scratched his scalp, and his blond curls jumped around.

'Oh, you went quite far, then.'

'Well, you know, nothing cool happens around here.'

'A couple of them came over, or just one?' Christine had noticed some vaguely tinted lip balm on one of the glasses. It was a little too much for a man. Henrik obviously understood that Christine was referring to the glasses on the table.

'Yeah, Zoey had wine, Tom and Al had a beer. They'll be there tonight. They're really looking forward to finally meet you. They've heard about you for months now.'

'It will be nice to finally meet them, although I must admit I don't know that much about them. Can you give me a crash course of who is who?' Christine asked with faked enthusiasm. The truth was she was really nervous. She had barely spoken to Henrik the last six months, and when she had been able to get a hold of him, he never wanted to speak about work or the crew.

Instead of answering her, he poured her a glass of wine.

'I don't know if I'm going tonight.' Henrik walked towards the big window next to the door. He pulled away the curtains and looked out.

'What do you mean, don't you want to go?' Christine spoke in a low voice and tried to hug him from behind.

'I just don't feel like it. It's just a lot of fuss and stress. Can't we just stay here and watch a film or something?' Christine knew this behaviour so well, and she knew she had to tread carefully.

'Well, I have barely seen you for the last six months, so there is nothing I want more than to just be with you alone. But I did come to London to be by your side for this premiere, so I would be sorry if we missed it.' Christine spoke slowly and carefully to him.

'It is a pretty awesome thing, and a big day in your life.'

He didn't answer.

'Are you nervous, sweetie?' She folded her arms around his waist and leaned her head against his back. She could feel his short, shallow breaths.

'You have no idea what it's like!' Henrik suddenly shouted as he pulled away from her.

'Your reputation is so important in this business, and it is so hard to get everything to work throughout the whole production. It is so many people, and one bad job from one of them can ruin everything I have worked for, for such a long time.' Henrik had turned his shouting into quiet desperation.

'You're right, I don't know what it's like at all.' Christine tried to keep herself calm. 'But, I do try to understand, and the more you tell me, the more I can help you, maybe.'

'I am telling you now, okay?' he was shouting again.

'Okay, we don't have to decide right this minute. The car will be here in half an hour, so before we decide whether to go or not, I think we should get ready, just in case. We can always stay on the sofa, but why don't we shower first? We can talk more about it while we clean you up. A shower will make you feel better.' She grabbed his arm and slowly led him up the stairs.

*

A text lit up Christine's phone:

Your driver has arrived.

Christine was on her way down the stairs. Henrik was sitting on a chair, in a suit. His crisp white shirt was open, revealing a hint of his sun kissed chest. His head was bowed towards the floor.

'Wow, don't you look great!' Christine kissed him on his forehead. 'You look like you should have been starring in the film!' He looked at her quickly and smiled. Then his gaze returned to the floor again. Christine knelt down in front of him and tried to make eye contact.

'I want to be here for you, Henrik. This is exactly why I am here. I will be right here, next to you all night if you need me to. We can leave before the viewing has started if you want to as well.' She stroked his head and continued:

'I am here for you. I don't really know much about the film, and I don't know that much about how the process has been, but I am here now. When you have been working on this film, you know I have only been a phone call away. You know I always answer. I think this production has gone pretty well, because you haven't had much need to speak to me.' She stroked his head, and then ran her fingers through his hair and continued:

'I am actually a bit surprised that you wanted me here tonight, but I understand that you needed me, just in case. If all these things I say now make you angry, I don't have to go with you. This isn't my dream or my career, but yours. So, we'll do whatever you want, Henrik.'

He finally lifted his head and looked at her.

'I am sorry for being an idiot. This year's World's Worst Boyfriend Award goes to yours truly,' he sighed. Christine replied with a kiss on his cheek: 'I know this year has been pretty special for us, but I do hope I will see you more next year. I only want the best for you, always. The first thing I do in the mornings is trying to call you, and it's the last thing I do before I go to sleep.'

'I need you tonight, Christine. Promise me you will be next to me tonight.' He looked deeply into her eyes. She grabbed his hand, and he pulled himself up from the chair.

'Of course,' she replied quietly.

The Art of Being a Leading Lady

They had been waiting in the car for a while, so when the driver asked her if she was ready, Christine had forgotten where she was. She took a second to focus, and looked in mirror in front of her. She gathered her hair to one side, and made sure she had closed her bag properly. She nodded to Henrik to show him that she was ready. The door on Henrik's side opened, and the flashes started to go off.

'This is madness!' Christine exclaimed. Henrik stared at her intensely. She squeezed his hand, and he took a deep breath. Then he turned his head to the flashes and stepped out of the car. There was an increase in the media's excitement, and the sound got more intense. Christine could hear young girls scream Henrik's name. She was surprised that young girls would scream the director's name, but on the other hand, she knew he was better looking than the actors. Before the car door opened, she took a deep breath. Henrik waited for her, and she accepted his hand. Her own hands were sweaty, and she nearly slipped on her heels, as they were an inch too tall for her. Christine had thought she would go under the radar with her outfit, but apparently being the date of Henrik was a big deal. She had no idea he would get this much attention. In addition to wearing some very high heels, Christine had put on a tailored black suit. It looked like she had nothing underneath her jacket, but her small breasts were securely taped in place. Christine had always been pretty flat chested, and Heidi had convinced her that this was a very cool look for her. Christine had made sure there was no possibility that her jacket would unbutton. Her green heels and green bag was a nod to Henrik's jungle film, because that was almost everything Christine knew about it. She had promised Heidi her earrings afterward as a present for all of her help, as they were the only thing that would fit her. Christine knew that her friend had almost died with jealousy that she when she had learned that Henrik's film would premier in Leicester Square in London, and that Christine would walk the red carpet along with Zoey James, the new Hollywood starlet. Zoey was from acting royalty, both her parents where famous, and she had had a privileged upbringing in Richmond. She was also the new face of a famous perfume company, among other wondrous endorsements and deals. The camera flashes continued, and Christine walked slowly up the carpet with Henrik. She was so glad he was there to hold her hand. Christine smiled, and tried to relax, and focused on not tripping. All of a sudden, the flashes turned, not focusing on them any longer. It was another car that had pulled up, most likely Zoey. She didn't really have a big part in the film, as there was no female in the book it was based on. Zoey had accepted a small role after Henrik had met her at some bar or something like that, Christine hadn't actually gotten the details of how Henrik had managed to persuade Zoey to join the cast.

Zoey was apparently well-trained to handle the press. As she stepped out of the car, Christine was almost shocked by her dress. It was a massive light-coloured tulle gown, almost angelic. The skirt was almost floating along the red carpet, but it was still very light, and see-through, Zoey's long thin legs showed through the fabric, and even a hint of a nipple. The dress was embroidered with bugs, which triumphed Christine's jungle theme without question. The invasion of bugs also made the dress less pretty and gave it an edge. Her strawberry-red hair was both messy and beautifully curled at the same time. Zoey was posing like she hadn't done anything but that since she was born. Christine's smile finally turned into a real one. She was so relieved the spotlight was off her and Henrik. It was almost strange how invisible she suddenly was on a red carpet. Christine felt her shoulders relax and she knew without a doubt which setting she preferred. Henrik's arm was pulling her in the direction of some journalists. Christine knew he was ordered to stop there. He was suddenly bombarded with questions.

'Are you nervous, Henrik?' one of the reporters asked him. 'When will we see you in front of the camera as well?' another asked. 'How was it to work with Zoey? Who is your leading lady?' came another. 'Why did you chose to adapt this book to the screen?' And finally, 'were you drawn to the parallels of the story and your own life?' Henrik's answers were polite and reflected. He was charming and confident. The nerves he had earlier was completely gone. He was charming and fun like he always was in public. Some journalists wanted Henrik in front of the movie poster. He let go of Christine's hand, and Zoey walked up to him as well. He slipped his hand around her tiny waist, as if it was the most natural thing for him to do. They posed together, just the two of them, and they looked like Hollywood royalty, like the new power couple.

Afterwards, some of the other actors joined them, but Zoey and Henrik were glued together. Christine didn't want to stare at them, but she found it a bit uncomfortable having Henrik so close to someone's almost-bare nipples. She didn't know where else to go, so she continued inside. Although Christine felt it was a bit weird to go inside without Henrik, if she was honest, she didn't mind too much. When she thought about it, she was used to going places by herself, and she always got less attention when she was with Henrik. She realised she was actually quite comfortable on her own. Christine approached the snack counter where she picked up a box of popcorn and a soda. She looked at the names on the film's poster, and was a bit embarrassed that she didn't know who they were, except for Henrik and Zoey. Suddenly, someone stopped by her.

'Hi! I thought I should introduce myself. I'm Alex. You're Henrik's girlfriend, right? Lovely to meet you.' The man was tall and thin, and he had the kind of beard that never seemed like it would be fashionable again, like something out of a historical photo. His suit was in the same category: wool, with a high waist, a waistcoat, and suspenders. He had a bow tie, and had spent some time waxing his moustache.

'Christine,' she said as she reached out her hand. Christine did recognise his name, and remembered it was one of the names Henrik had mentioned earlier that day. 'Nice to meet you.'

'So, you know, when Henrik and I get together, we never talk about our private life,' Alex said. 'So, you have to fill me in. Have you two been dating for long?' The fact that Henrik never spoke about her, didn't surprise her. On the other hand, she didn't know that much about his work either.

'Yes, we've been together for twelve years actually,' she said. 'We got together when we were very young.'

'Good God, you're practically married then. You must be quite used to Henrik's travels and projects I assume.'

'I am actually quite used to him being away. But I know it means so much to him, and I have always supported his work.'

'You should visit us on set for the next film! It's busy, and we're always moving on to the next location, but we always find time for some social gathering almost every night.' Christine had no idea Henrik was planning another movie already, and certainly not that he was planning another one with this Alex she was speaking to. She gave a polite smile but didn't feel like smiling at all. She felt so out of place, and knew she should have prepared better, but there had been no time for that. The bell was ringing, and they had to find their seats.

'Lovely to meet you, Alex,' Christine said as she was about to walk into the theatre. She stopped by the door and waited for Henrik. She had already had a few big sips from her paper cup of soda, and she thought she should have taken the time to go to the bathroom. Henrik finally arrived with the actors.

'Henrik,' she called as he passed the door.

'Oh, right, there you are. Are you ready? Our seats should be at the front, so we have to go through that entrance.'

Henrik didn't grab her hand. Christine felt that he had almost forgotten her, that it was more of a surprise to see her, that he had not been looking for her. It felt like he didn't need her at all. Throughout the years, they had seen many films together, and many films that Henrik had created. He had always made a thing of showing them, a small premiere in their own living room, whether it was a small clip of something, or one of the longer ski films. He was always nervous to show them, and Christine usually started by saying that she was very proud of him, and that she knew it would be amazing because he was so talented.

This was his first feature film, and for the first time, Christine didn't know what to expect. It was the first time that he hadn't really involved her in the process at all, except for the fact that she had read the book the film was based on a couple of years ago. She knew that Henrik had a dark side that he only dared to show her, and she knew that this project was harder for him emotionally than his skiing films. He had always been fascinated with films with an anti-hero, someone that had some sort of personal struggle, a character that he somehow identified with. She knew that in this film, he had finally dared to use that side of him, and she knew that was also the reason that he hadn't discussed it with her at all.

She said nothing this time when they sat down, because this time, she didn't know what to say.

Throughout the film, she held Henrik's hand. He didn't look at her once, nor did he squeeze it back like he usually did. As for the story, Christine enjoyed the additions Henrik had made. He had managed to portray the main character exactly how she imagined him from the novel. The main character had left a very good, materialistic life in the search for something else, and ended up as a guide in the jungle in Bolivia. The character felt empty and incapable of loving, and he affair with Zoey felt very much a part of the story, as he tried to love her, but didn't really love her at all.

Christine didn't want to think too much about the parallels to Henrik's life. It felt too close to his story in some ways, or what his story could have been if he had run away at some point. Although she had read the book herself, the storyline hit her a lot harder when it was Henrik who had adapted it into the big screen. In every poetic clip, every soundtrack, every word spoken, she knew he was behind it, as they were all him. This was his work in every way possible.

She knew Henrik was very talented, but it hurt her that his best film was made without her present in his life. She also thought that the film showed that it was good for Henrik to do something completely different from his father. It was the only way to not be compared with him.

After the credits had rolled, Christine realised she still had tears in her eyes, although she had stopped thinking about the film a while ago. She squeezed Henrik's hand once again, leaned towards him and said, "I am so incredibly proud of you."

Finally, he looked at her, and he was pale. She squeezed his hand once more. He smiled. The lights came on. As the applause started, Henrik let go of her hand.

Feeling Like a Bond Girl

There were loud cheers of support and admiration as Henrik walked into the lounge. The waitresses were all in hot pink jumpsuits, and the room was very cosy and nice. More cosy than fancy, Christine thought. She had expected a more grandiose place considering Heidi's reaction when she told her friend the name of the hotel the afterparty would be at. Heidi had said it was *the* place to spot celebrities, and that it was amazing that they would host the afterparty. She had said that it was a sign of how famous Henrik had become. *No, that's how famous Zoey James has become*, Christine had thought at the time. The shouting came from a group at the bar. Henrik smiled and walked straight up to them, politely smiling and nodding to the people he passed who tried to talk to him. Christine followed him, her hand in his.

When they arrived at the bar, she waited for Henrik to introduce her to everyone. His hand slipped. She stood there smiling, but he didn't introduce her to anyone, not even a group introduction. She knew he had forgotten her already. Christine tried to tell herself that it was a good thing, that she was happy for him. Henrik was no longer nervous, and the evening was going better than she knew he had expected. She turned towards the bar instead, acting like it was the bar she had been aiming for the whole time, and not the group of people.

Once she was by the counter, she looked around the room. Her shoes had started to hurt, so Christine leaned backwards a little on the heels to give her the balls of her feet a rest. Zoey had entered, having changed into a very short, sequinned dress. It was silver and warrior-like, with structured shoulders. She probably couldn't sit in that dress, but her legs looked endlessly long, although she had quite a petite figure.

For the first time this evening, Christine felt like her job was done, the pressure was off. She finally had time to observe the room properly and think about how surreal the night had been already. There were several faces she recognised, so she could assume they were celebrities of some sort. She felt like she had stumbled in on something she should clearly back away from. It was so strange that her boyfriend, Henrik, was the reason for this surreal gathering of celebrities and other known people. She felt she did not belong there at all, and neither did she want to. She was, of course, fascinated with the girls like Zoey that were there. She didn't want to *be* like Zoey at all, it was more her need of attention that fascinated her, it must be exhausting to crave it all the time, like an addictive drug. *Maybe Henrik was starting to be addicted to it as well?* She herself was enjoying being invisible by herself at the bar.

She felt her shoulders relax, the muscles in her neck loosening, and she thought to herself that no one there would care if she had a great night or a bad night, or who she spoke to. She noticed a song she really loved was playing. She closed her eyes, and slowly started to sing along quietly with her head moving from side to side.

Christine looked in the mirror behind the bar. All of a sudden, there was a familiar face amongst the crowd, smiling at her. *Oh no, he has seen me.* It was Charlie. She had barely seen him since they had walked home from the concert together last year. She had seen him go past her office on the way to Harald's a few times, and he had stood a few times in the foyer talking for a while. Christine hadn't spoken to him on these occasions, nor had she made proper eye contact with him either. She had been quite shocked at how much she had opened up to him, without knowing him at all, and had therefore been avoiding him on purpose. Maybe it was because he was a stranger that it was so easy to talk to him that night, but she hadn't thought about how it would be to meet him again at work, with everyone else around. Therefore, it had just been easier to avoid him. ... *And now, he is on his way to speak to me..*

She continued to look behind the bar, but from the corner of her eye, she could see him getting closer. She pretended to look for the drinks, but she dreaded the moment he would be there. The only thing worse than having no one to hang with, was people you knew - knowing it. Christine continued to avoid the reflections in the mirror: her lonely self and the presence of him.

But then, there he was, right behind her, speaking to her in the mirror: 'I thought by the time I got over here I would know what to say. And all I could think about was that anything I would be saying would an improvement on last year, when I asked about the condition of you bum.'

Christine looked in the mirror and saw those blue eyes looking at her. She found Charlie's smile comforting. She turned around and gave him a polite kiss on each cheek. "So, which other things did you prepare that were so bad you decided repeating last year was the best alternative?"

'Ah,' he sighed. 'Let me give you a recap of what when through my head. First one was "lovely to see you again, *Miss Loveness*".' He pronounced her last name in the English way.

'Ah, sweet and definitely been used before…' She wrinkled her brow, looking forward to the next line.

'Oh, it gets better - or worse. It depends on how you look at it, I suppose. How about: you look so hot I would say you were arm *chilli* instead of arm *candy* tonight!"' Charlie started laughing almost before he had finished the line.

'Wow that was pretty awful, you should be glad I've already met you.' They both laughed.

Charlie became more serious as his laugh subsided. 'The other one was …' He was paused and looked down. 'Well, I was going to say something like "I hope I am not the first one to say you look amazing tonight."

Christine didn't even want to think about if his words were really true or not, and instead instinctively answered: 'Thank you, that was sweet. That was the best one.'

'Wait, not done yet!' He was more spirited than before. "I was going to say, 'you look amazing tonight … and freakishly tall!" Charlie grinned at her. Being quite tall himself, he was apparently not used to already very tall girls in very high heels.

'Thanks. I guess …' Christine didn't know if it was a compliment or not, but by the look of his grin, she knew Charlie liked her height. 'I am only here for moral support, you know. I am glad I didn't have to dress for maximum attention tonight.'

Charlie leaned in towards Christine's ear and whispered: 'Well, you deserve maximum attention anyway.' He then looked over at Henrik, who was clearly having a ball with a very loud Zoey. Christine knew what he meant, without looking towards Henrik. She could hear Zoey's laughter over the buzz in the room and the lounge music.

'I would have been very proud if you were my arm candy tonight.' Charlie had pulled back from Christine's ear, and was now looking straight into her eyes.

She was completely caught off guard with his statement. She turned around and leaned against the bar. 'You don't look so bad yourself,' Christine replied after a few seconds, trying to avoid the direct attention from Charlie.

'Come on, I look like a teacher next to you. I don't know what to do when there isn't a defined dress code, which clearly results in this outfit.' Charlie was wearing a white shirt, jeans, a wool blazer and nice shoes, like every other posh Englishman would in London.

'So, tell me, *Miss Loveness*, is this part of your usual everyday life? Jetting off for premieres all over the world?' Christine quite liked that he addressed her in a formal way.

'Not at all. This must be more *your* life, going to premieres and lavish parties, using seedy, cliché pickup lines to get a new girl in bed every other night, living your marvellous London life as a financial wonder boy?' Christine returned the question, and was surprised that she managed to look directly into his eyes the whole time.

'Well, I guess I should get more used to this, really, as I am actually the chairman of the production company. You know, one of the perks that comes with being Harald's representative in London.'

'Does this production firm invest in films other than Henrik's?'

'I have no idea. I was put up as chairman since yesterday. I haven't looked into it yet, but I am assuming this isn't a profitable company just yet. Actually, my friend Max composed the music, so a few of my friends are here as well. Otherwise, I don't think I would have shown up. I don't think Henrik meant for anyone from the office to actually attend.'

'Oh, so your friends are here?' Christine was disappointed that he wasn't attending alone, like she felt she was. 'Where are they? I want them to tell me all the embarrassing stories about you that they know.'

Christine started scouting the room. Were his friends as polished and perfect as he? Or was he a more genuine guy with nerdy friends?

Charlie clearly got a bit nervous, and she knew he was thinking that his friends would reflect on him.

'They're over there,' Charlie was pointing at a group of sofas and comfortable seats, where Christine could spot three typical Englishmen. They did stand out a bit, as they were all wearing striped or checked shirts and jackets, and they were definitely less trendy than the rest of the guests.

'Should we join them? The stories they will tell you are of course not true, by the way,' he smiled mischievously.

'I'd love to, but I have to give Henrik his drink first.' The drinks she had ordered at the bar before Charlie had come over appeared to be ready, and Christine remembered that she had to pretend that she had ordered for Henrik as well.

'Okay, just come on over whenever you want. You know where to find me,' Charlie said as she left. Christine felt relieved Charlie was there. Christine started to walk towards Henrik with the two drinks. As she approached, she placed one of the drinks on a table and touched Henrik's shoulder. He turned around and smiled.

'Hey, there you are!' Henrik said, as if he had actually missed her. She pointed at the drink, and he gave her a big kiss on the check. As soon as Henrik had picked up his drink, he turned around and continued the conversation he was in the middle of. Christine stood there, looking at the ground, feeling completely rejected. Not knowing what to do with herself, should she just leave again, as if she was just a waitress? All of a sudden, a hand was in front of her, and when she looked up, a guy with big hair in a plain white t-shirt was ready to greet her. 'Hi, I'm Tom, the production manager.'

'Christine, Henrik's girlfriend.' She regretted saying that the moment it came out. *Had Henrik told his friends about me? Or would this be as awkward as it was with Al earlier?*

'Ah, the mysterious girlfriend, we were wondering if you were made up. The few times Henrik has talked about you, you sound too good to be true … and you know, you never came on set … but here you are! Clearly existing! And most likely too good for him!' Tom laughed. 'What I means is, I know you are a very patient and unselfish girlfriend.'

Christine was smiling, but it wasn't real. She was only being polite. *What did he mean by that? Was Henrik so selfish, that to be with him I have to be the opposite?* Christine felt even worse than she had before. *Does everyone think I am stupid to put up with Henrik?*

She was pushed by someone and bumped into Tom. She smiled as she moved away from him, embarrassed to have had her cleavage almost in his face.

'So why don't you spent more time in London? It would be nice to get to know the girl Henrik has been attached to for all these years.' Tom clearly wanted to continue the conversation.

Henrik was standing next to them, and Christine knew that he could hear their conversation.

'Well, I do have a job in Oslo,' Christine started to explain.

'That's not really a problem, is it? I am sure you would find something to do here in London as well.' Tom was obviously hinting at the fact that Henrik certainly did not have to work for a living, and for that matter, neither did she. Christine was in shock at how indiscreet this Tom was, it was certainly not any of his business. Christine knew by his bluntness that he couldn't be British, and she did sense another accent as well.

'Well, I like spending time in Oslo, and Henrik likes to travel. It's not like he's in London all the time, either.'

Christine knew that Henrik overheard their conversation, and she was hoping he would interrupt. Instead, she saw that Henrik was slowly moving away from them. A guy suddenly interrupted them, someone was obviously close to Tom. Before Tom had turned around to introduce Christine, she had already left. *Why do I even try?* Christine thought to herself. She looked around the room. There were so many people, and Christine didn't know any of them. She had met a few of Henrik's friends from university, but she couldn't recognise any of them, if any of them were even present at all.

Christine looked towards the area where Charlie's friends where. He was sitting on the armrest of a lounge chair and drinking a beer, but it didn't look like he was completely following the story of his friend. It didn't take long before Charlie noticed that Christine was looking in his direction. He jumped off the armrest of the lounge chair and started to walk towards her. She wasn't afraid of him any longer and walked towards him.

'Hi,' he said when they were in talking distance. 'Do you want to meet everyone?'

Christine felt a great sense of relief: 'That would be very nice.'

One by one, he introduced his friends to her as his colleague from the Oslo office. He left out the "this is the girlfriend of the director" part or "this is my boss' daughter-in-law" so she could avoid questions about her relationship. If they had watched her in the theatre, they would have known. However, they were most likely were walking the red carpet themselves, and therefore didn't notice anyone other than the big stars. Compared to them, she was a tad overdressed, but this was London, and they were probably used to girls dressing over the top. They made room for her in the sofa, right in the middle. Christine felt like the centre of attention and liked it for once. There were plenty of anecdotes and side-stories to accompany the introductions, and Christine was enjoying the show, it was quite entertaining. It was obvious they all knew each other very well, and that they didn't take themselves too seriously at all.

Ben, who was on Christine right hand, started whispering

funny little jokes about them in her ear, like 'Charlie needed bedwetter sheets until last year" and "Louis can't keep a girlfriend, but it's hard, you know, when you only want to date women over eighty.'

After the jokes and introductions were over, he started speaking of their friendship.

'I'm Charlie's best and oldest friend. I bet he hasn't told you about me, because he must be a bit embarrassed of me.' Ben said it all with a smile, and Christine sensed he must be one of the rare types that was full of humour and great spirits, and turned everything that was difficult to talk about into something funny.

'Don't worry, I don't know Charlie that well, so I am sure your name would have come up eventually.'

'Let me fill you in: I was cool, he was a nerd. He had these weird glasses, and he never cleaned them. I was rich, he wasn't. Even our maid had a nicer car than the sewing machine of a car Charlie arrived in every morning. The rest of us knew that our future was taken care of, so we were quite relaxed. So while little Charlie was reading his books, the rest of us were planning pranks to pull on him. So while Charlie is doing great, I spend my days at a crappy office with no windows, where I really don't know what I am actually doing. It's something with real estate, and we are supposed to develop something.'

'I am sure you're making it sound worse than it is, real estate development must be exciting.'

'The thing is, I don't think we actually develop any properties, since I have never seen any of the properties I am supposed to be developing. We seem to sell it all before something is even there, you know, physically. Either way, it's all a blur to me, and then I have my best friend on the front pages, and not just the financial papers, he was even in *Esquire* a few months ago. And he is mentioned in *Tatler* all the time, or so I have heard. I would never be caught dead reading that magazine. Although I do find the articles quite funny …' Christine was laughing. She could see from his smile that he was reading that magazine whenever he got his hands on it, but wouldn't admit it out loud.

'I am very proud of him though," Ben continued. 'Whereas I sit there every day and wonder if I am actually part of a huge scam - but I really don't want to know, to be honest. II just hope I won't be locked in, I attending my own wedding summer.'

'Wow, congratulations! I guess that's one way of putting it.. I assume you are not in charge of planning?' Christine exclaimed.

'I thought that was the only field where I was beating Charlie. He used to be terrible with girls. And then he drags you in here, it makes me *hate* him.'

'Oh, that's a strong word.'

'Why does Charlie have to rub in my face all the beautiful Scandinavian supermodels he hangs with?'

"It's just tons of make up. Tell me about the girl you are marrying!"

" I do think she is marrying me for tax purposes, but then again, I need her to keep my mother away."Christine was still laughing. This was so different from earlier in the evening. She was enjoying herself. Christine looked over at Charlie, who was next to Ben, but leaning forward for a conversation with a friend on the end. She was so glad he had come up to her.

Ben continued: 'The thing is, it really hit me hard, you know, the *"love"* thing. Have you been hit by it yet?' He caught her looking at Charlie. Christine didn't know what she should say, she was really surprised that he asked her such a question. *Should I say yes? Does he know I am with Henrik, or would lead him to think that I am in love with Charlie? Should I say yes and quickly add that I am seeing Henrik? What did it really mean, to be hit by "love"?*

Before she had the time to reply, Charlie joined in all of a sudden.

"Good God, Ben, stop it with the personal questions. Can't I bring you anywhere in public?" Charlie was clearly listening and had understood that Christine was uncomfortable.

'I am just trying to be your "wingman" here, and I am trying to figure out whether she is single or not. She is *clearly* out of your league; she is the closest I have come across to a Bond girl. She is a foreign supermodel but has the brains of a scientist, and for once I thought you might need some help here. The ones you can handle on your own usually look like something the cat dragged in.' Christine noticed that Charlie was blushing and trying to give Ben a stern look.

'So, what time are you leaving tomorrow? I'm assuming you're going back for the Christmas dinner.' Charlie was trying to change the subject, while Ben sat there quite smug, obviously happy that he managed to embarrass his best friend. Christine smiled.

'I think I will be on the ten o'clock flight from Heathrow, it depends if Henrik is joining me or not.' As she said Henrik's name, Christine remembered that she hadn't talked to him in a while. She looked around and couldn't see him, nor could she see anyone he had been around him all night either - not Alex, not Tom and definitely not Zoey. Christine was wondering where he was. *Could he really just leave me here?*

'Please excuse me, I have to leave.' Christine jumped up from the sofa, and the others let her get up quickly. Christine had barely left the table when she felt a tap on her shoulder.

'There's no point of leaving already, please stay?' It was Charlie, who was looking quite surprised that she had all of a sudden decided to leave. He had gotten up right after her.

'Yes, I'm sorry. Thanks for being a great friend tonight,' she said, and gave him just one kiss on the check. Charlie looked like he didn't know what more to say, without offending her or her relationship. The guys behind him started yelling. 'The night has only just begun!'

'Let us know next time you're in London!' Christine waved and smiled at them. On her way out to the entrance, she got her phone out, and called Henrik. It went right to voicemail. She started to write him a text instead.

Where are you? Give me a ring, I can't get through. C

When she got to the entrance, Christine started to look for a black cab.

'Christine!'

She heard Charlie's voice behind her again. He tried to look relaxed, but she knew he must have walked quite quickly.

'Hey, I just wanted to say that I can have my driver pick you up tomorrow if you like, you know, unless you are not on the same flight as Henrik.' At that moment, a taxi stopped, and Christine opened the door.

'Thanks. Bye, Charlie, see you tomorrow then.' Christine looked at him through the window as the taxi left, but all she could think about was Henrik.

*

Christine found the key to the door in her small bag. There was no light inside, so Henrik probably wasn't there either. She opened the door.

'Henrik?' There was no answer. She found her phone.

I am going to bed. C

*

A beam of light through the curtains woke Christine up.

She looked at her phone. 05:49. One message from Henrik.

Where are you? Was just at the bar in the basement. Joining the crew for a night cap, will be home shortly. H

She looked at the time the message had been sent. 1:44.

Christine laid her head back on the pillow and looked at the ceiling. After a while, she took up her phone, and dialled Henrik.

'Christine! Hi!'

'Hi sweetie, where are you?'

'Oh, I am on my way home now actually. Are you okay? I didn't hear from you.'

'I know. I went to bed. See you soon then. Love you.'

*

After a few minutes, Christine was woken up by Henrik.

'Hey, have you been on your phone? I actually bought a few newspapers.' Henrik was sitting on the bed at her side.

'No, I have only checked my messages. Are you sure they have written something already? And do you think it is a good idea to read it?'

She could barely open her eyes, but she started stroking his back. He smelt like a combination of sweat, alcohol and cigarettes.

'Where are the newspapers, then?'

'I left them on the table downstairs.'

'Let's go down then, and we can look at news sites down there as well.' She knew that Henrik didn't dare to read the critics without her. Through the window by the stairs, Christine could see out to the street. It looked like it was only their little house that had lights on. Christine put the kettle on once downstairs.

'Are you really ready for this?'

'Well, I can't avoid it forever. Eventually I will find out anyway.' Christine sat down next to him.

'True. Papers or websites first?'

Henrik started by opening a newspaper. 'Printed on paper is the worst. They are more permanent.'

Christine sat next to him and put her arm over his shoulder and let him sink down.

*

Christine woke up again.

She felt the moist London air come through the single glazing. She turned around to congratulate Henrik again on the great critics, but he wasn't there. *Seriously?* Christine couldn't believe it. He must have gone back to the party. She didn't even bother to text him. She wasn't mad, and she wasn't sad. She just felt numb. She started to pack her bag and then got into the shower. She hoped Henrik stayed away, that he didn't turn up at the airport drunk and smelly. She knew she had to go to the

Christmas party by herself, but she wasn't nearly as nervous as last year. The only thing she was dreading was having to explain why Henrik wasn't there. *Again.*

Nipples on a Front Page

Christine calmly walked through the corridors at Heathrow with her small carry-on suitcase in tow. In front of her she saw a newsstand with what appeared to be new magazines in the holder. *Should I buy one?* The press they had read that morning was mostly about the film. The reviews had been quite good and had praised Henrik as a producer and director. He had entered film industry and taken it by storm. In a way, it was a great relief.

Still Christine couldn't get the images from last night out of her head. The pictures of her were okay, but she felt that anyone could see that she wasn't comfortable. Henrik was beaming, and Zoey was the natural star she was. The papers they had read in the morning hours weren't the type of media that would mention too much gossip, but with Henrik staying out all night and the lip gloss from the night before, it all just gave Christine a bad feeling. She just didn't want to think about it, but she felt there was something going on. When Henrik had gotten home to read the newspapers, she just gone on autopilot, being there for him, as she knew how sensitive he was with any critique. Now that she was on her own, she could think about herself again. *Is this how my life will be in the future?* Maybe it would be okay if they were better at calling each other. Henrik had always been distant for longer periods, but it would always pass. It had never lasted as long as this time, and the times before he had always been a lot happier to spend time with her when they finally met, but it would pass.

Christine hadn't dared to look at the worst gossip pages, the ones that were much more interested in Zoey and Henrik's life than the film. Instead of picking up a newspaper, Christine picked up an older magazine and she ran thought it quickly to check that there wasn't a big article about Zoey in it. She tried to fit it into the front pocket of her carry-on, but it was too full. The suitcase was heavier than usual. She always had her laptop with her, but this time she had clothes for the dinner tonight. There were often delays in December, so she brought the outfit for tonight as well, in case she had to go directly from the airport to the dinner.

Harald had made sure there were rooms for them at the venue, so Christine also had time to mingle with guests who stayed over for breakfast. All her energy and focus had gone into the previous night, she had hardly checked if she had everything in her suitcase for tonight.

It was a strange feeling. She had hardly actually thought about the dinner tonight. Maybe it was because she was so much more comfortable than last year, and she knew what she was doing. The press would be there tonight as well, but she felt that she could handle it. Christine picked up her phone and rang Henrik. She had waited until she was at the airport on purpose. She knew that he must be so hung over, and quite frankly she didn't want him next to her tonight. She got along with her colleagues, and the presence of him would scare them away. Before she would never go anywhere without Henrik, and lately, she would rather go without him. It was a long while since he had felt like her best friend. Her phone rang for a long time, but there was no answer. She started to write a text.

Hi! I'm on my way to Oslo, boarding soon. I assume you returned to the party, would have preferred a heads-up or a text from you, but I hope you had a great celebration for your great reviews. I'm assuming you're not joining me in Oslo. No worries. I'm so proud of you. Sleep tight, and remember to eat. Will try to call you later. C.

She walked to the gate, and wrote another text to Henrik.

I hope to see you this weekend, and that you will spend the rest of December at home with me. Lots of love, C.

*

Christine was tired from the previous night. Usually, she stood in the background for boarding, but this time she used her card so she could be one of the first to board.

When seated, she took out her magazine, leaned her head against the headrest, and put her scarf in front of her face, so that it became completely dark. It was a nice way to avoid attention too. When she was half asleep, she could hear the flight attendant announce that the flight would be completely full, and that they should use space under their seat as well.

Christine could hear someone put their things on the seat next to her. She lifted the scarf off of her right eye and could see a phone and an iPad. She heard the sound of the seatbelt warning turn on, and she dozed off again. There was movement from the neighbouring seat. Christine could hear the storage compartment above her open. The scarf had fallen down, and she could sense daylight. She slightly opened one eye. Christine thought the man next to her was quite attractive, without being able to see his face. The man was still rummaging through his bag, obviously trying to find something that was lost deep within it. Christine couldn't help but notice his biceps through his shirt as his arms moved, his hands pushing things aside in the bag. When she opened her eyes properly, she almost jumped when she realised who it was next to her. *Charlie.*

'Hi,' he whispered.

'Hi,' she replied quietly.

'I am not stalking you. Coincidentally I got the seat next to you. I tried to change, but the flight is full. Don't mind me, just go back to sleep. Please.' Christine lifted her scarf and closed her eyes again.

*

The light was intense. Her scarf must have fallen down from her face. Christine looked out of the window. They were above a thick white layer of clouds. The sky was intensely blue, and she counted three white lines of planes that had passed them. She had slept through take off. She had been so tired she hadn't even closed the curtain. On the foldable table that was pulled down next to her, Christine saw a cup of coffee, a bottle of water, and an unopened box with food with a bread roll on top. The man next to her was holding an iPad was in front of the table, with a very nice watch on his wrist. He was looking at an online car magazine, and there where at least a few pictures of what looked like very expensive cars. His sleeves were rolled up, and the arms were quite tanned and manly. Christine suddenly remembered that it was Charlie who sat next to her - or had that been a dream? She moved her gaze to see his face, to check. It did look like Charlie. He didn't know she was awake, and his eyes were still on his iPad. She looked at his chin, chiselled and defined. His stubble was a day old, or maybe more. It was the kind of stubble blond men had trouble growing, because you needed dark, thick hair to grow a nice stubble in a day. A few grey hairs had appeared in his neatly trimmed sideburns. He lifted his hand and scratched his neck. He yawned and lifted his eyes towards Christine.

'Hi,' she whispered and smiled at him.

'Hi!' He seemed surprised to see her awake. 'I hope you slept well. I didn't want to wake you when they passed with food, so I set some aside for you, in case you wanted something. Don't feel obliged. It was just in case you were hungry.' He rambled on, like he seemed to do when he was a little nervous.

'Thanks, that's very sweet of you.'

Charlie smiled, and then his gaze returned to his iPad again, as if he wanted to leave her alone if she wanted. Christine opened the water bottle, and drank half of it in one go. She ate a bit of a bread roll, and drank her coffee, while looking at Charlie's iPad. He was now reading something that looked a lot more serious, like the *Economist* or something. She couldn't help but smile at the fact that he was maybe trying to impress her. She opened a little box of chocolates.

'Do you want a bite?' She held the box towards him.

'Thanks, but no thanks. I'm not sure whether I'll fit into my shirt tonight or not, and those will not help.'

'You're sure?'

'I'm sure. Unless you want me to repeat your no-shirt look from last night instead.' Christine started laughing with her mouth filled with chocolate. The thought of Charlie appearing at the ball without a shirt and a bowtie around his neck was hilarious. 'If you turn up without a shirt tonight, they will think you're some sort of entertainment, or depending on the amount of chest hair or abs, think you were a mental patient."

Charlie snorted: 'I can assure you, I will look like I should have been in an institution.'

'Are you done looking at cars?' she asked mockingly.

'Ah, yes.' he mumbled, while his neck turned red. 'I guess I am done trying to appear serious.' He went back to the webpage with cars and smiled. Christine took up her magazine and started to look through it. It was nice to have Charlie next to her. She flipped through the magazine, but she wasn't actually that interested. She always liked to start at the back, so she could skip all of the pages with commercials. On one of the last pages, with photos from different event and parties, Christine saw Henrik's face. It was an event for a fashion brand in London. Christine didn't know he attended those things. She looked at who else was there. All of a sudden, she saw Zoey's face next to the designer. Christine quickly put the magazine in the folder at the wall in front of her. She didn't know what to think. Two hundred people must have been there, but she just didn't like the coincidence. She looked out the window instead. After a while, Charlie leaned towards her without looking at her. 'I got a rental car ready at the airport. Do you want a ride?'

Christine had planned to take the train, but had no excuse not to accept. 'Thanks, that would be great. Are you heading directly to the office?'

'Yes, I'm not sure how much time I will have there, though. I thought I might go up to Lysebu a bit early to see the sunset. I want to see the place before it gets dark.'

'Excellent idea,' Christine looked out the window again. They had passed the heavy clouds beneath them, and Christine felt she could see half of Norway lit up with bright winter sun. Everything was covered in snow, just like a postcard. She was looking forward to going up to Lysebu, and she was hoping it would stay clear. It was so nice to feel the sunlight hit her face through the tiny window, and she imagined how nice it could be tomorrow as well. She wondered if she should bring her cross-country skies with her but thought she might not have the time before check-out.

'Looks like we will be on time. I brought all my stuff with me for tonight in case we were delayed.' Christine spoke to Charlie without looking at him.

'So did I, since I don't have a permanent place in Oslo. Are you staying at the hotel as well?'

'Yes, I thought it would be nice to wake up there tomorrow morning, it is such a magical place. You should definitely go up there early today.'

'You're more than welcome to join me.'

'Thanks for the offer, I'll consider it.'

Christine thought about the fact that Charlie hadn't asked her at all about last night, or where Henrik was. Maybe Charlie had seen him after she had left. She didn't dare to bring it up.

*

Charlie took Christine's carry-on down from the baggage compartment above their seats, without them exchanging much more than a "thank you". She was calm in his presence, and she didn't feel the need to keep a polite conversation going. Like they were old friends. They walked together through the shop area, still not saying anything.

After a while, Charlie wanted to buy some things for the ride, and Christine waited for him by the entrance. While she waited, she looked at the day's newspapers and gossip magazines. There she was, on the front page. She was standing there with Henrik, with the biggest picture of Zoey next to them. "Love triangle!" was the heading. On another magazine was a picture of Henrik and Zoey, his arm around her. There was a smaller picture of her alone next to them. The heading was "Will they be Hollywood's Next IT Couple? " Christine couldn't deny it. Henrik and Zoey did look like the new Brad Pitt and Angelina Jolie. Zoey was beaming, her grin covering the whole page. Christine couldn't move. She just stood there. She had thought something similar, but it was another thing to have it spelled out to her on a gossip magazine. Ever since Henrik and Zoey were pictured playing in a pool with the rest of the crew earlier that year, Christine had had her suspicions, like the rest of the world, apparently. Or Norway, at least, but that *felt* like the whole world. Suddenly, Christine could feel something pulling her arm. It was Charlie. She just stood there, while he tried to gently signal that they should leave. She finally managed to say something.

'Can you buy these for me?'

'Are you sure that's a good idea?' Charlie tried to look her in the eyes, but her gaze was fixed on the magazines.

'Yes, I need to know what they say, and what everyone is thinking. I usually avoid these, but I need to know if those headlines are just to sell papers, or if there is more to it.'

"They are always trying to make more out of things than there really is, but if you really want to read them, I will go inside and buy them for you.' Charlie still sounded quite sceptical. She nodded and felt a sudden need to leave.

'I have to go to the ladies, so can you meet me over there?' Christine was looking towards the bathrooms.

'Sure, I'll take your luggage. Are you all right?' Charlie was looking concerned, but before he got an answer, Christine was already on her way. She walked as fast as she could without running, pulling up the lapels on her coat, so no one would recognise her. Luckily, she never wore anything that stood out, her height drew enough attention. She kept her gaze down, while her stomach turned, and her pulse was rising. She felt warm, and feverish. The sweat was starting to bead on her forehead. She pushed the door open. There was fortunately no queue. With both hands she pushed one cubicle door open, and managed to lock it quickly. Christine barely made it to the toilet bowl before the coffee and the chocolates came up. She stayed there, on her knees, with her hands leaning against the toilet bowl. She breathed heavily. After a while, she sat back, leaning against the door.

*

While Charlie put the bags in the boot of the car, Christine was on her phone, checking some of the gossip sites online. She dared to start with the worst of them, as she wanted to look at the one that had posted the picture of Henrik and Zoey in the pool. It was the first major article Henrik was mentioned in in a British paper, most likely since Zoey had been followed by the paparazzi for a while. Or, perhaps she had called the paparazzi, as Heidi had told her that was usual for attention-seeking celebrities. "Frolicking Friends" was the headline.. In the picture, Zoey sat on Henrik's shoulders, playing with a ball in the pool with two others. Christine normally didn't read that site, but Heidi, who read it daily, came to her with it to her. Christine didn't like it at all, but Heidi had tried to comfort her, telling her that it was not too bad, that it was nice that Henrik's film was getting some publicity at least, but that maybe she should talk to Henrik about it and how it made her feel. Christine had, of course, avoided that conversation. This time around, Christine found it a lot worse. There was no pool and Zoey was not on Henrik's shoulders, but

Christine had been there, and Henrik had not cared about her at all. With these new headlines, she felt that the whole world knew that he was a bad boyfriend. But she had no proof that he was cheating, and it could all be made up. Christine wanted to call Heidi, but she was afraid that if Heidi thought it was bad, it really *was* bad. The British news had mainly focused on Zoey's dress, not who she was pictured next to. In one article, Henrik was described as the pool hunk, and the heir-director. One of the articles said that Zoey had tried to hide her terrible acting by showing off her nipples. Christine was relieved. She lifted her eyes from her phone and noticed that they were already out of the parking garage, and on the road.

'How are you doing?' Charlie asked. She had forgotten he was beside her. *How did I get from the restrooms to his car? Was he there when I was sick?*

She didn't answer his question and instead asked one of her own.

'Where are the Norwegian magazines?' She tried to look in the backseat.

'I put them in the door next to you. I thought you might want to flip through them afterwards.' She noticed out of the corner of her eye that he took a quick look at her. Christine could feel the saltiness from the tears on her face. She knew she looked awful.

She picked up the first magazine, with the heading "What a Love Triangle!" in a bold type.

She skimmed through. "Film premiere... London... Henrik ... fortune ... Zoey's dress ... Henrik's long-term love had taken the trip to London to be by his side on his big day ... not dating the films leading lady."   That was it. Christine turned the page quickly. *That was it? With THAT heading?* She opened another magazine. "Hollywood's new super couple ... premiere... London ... Henrik's first feature film ... Henrik's fortune ... Zoey's transparent dress ... would love to work with Henrik again ... Are they the new perfect director-actress combo?" *Was that it? Was that what they meant? Super "couple" was actually super "combination"?* Christine read through all of the magazines and the newspapers. It was all very innocent. She read through them all once more, to make sure she hadn't missed something between the lines. She took a deep breath and felt her shivering hand starting to rest. She looked straight ahead, without looking at anything. There was a field in front of them, and the snow lay on it like a perfect blanket. In the middle of the field stood a large, old oak. The branches were covered in a thin layer of snow. It was very cold, so the snow had also turned into large crystals. The tree was sparkling in the winter sun. Christine took another deep breath and closed her eyes. So it was nothing. Nothing to worry about. Nothing that really implied anything, at least. It was only tabloid headlines to sell papers. *Why don't I feel more relieved?* She was relieved that her suspicion wasn't all over the papers, but she that didn't mean it wasn't true. The feelings she had didn't go away just because the word *cheating* wasn't mentioned in the papers. Even though she might have overreacted it didn't mean it wasn't true.

'Are you all right?' Charlie put his hand on her sleeve. She took another deep breath.

'I'm all right.'

'Do you want to talk about it?'

'No.'

'What did you actually think the papers had written? My Norwegian is extremely limited, but did they say anything different from than the British ones?'

'No, I just didn't like the headings.'

'Understandable, I googled translated those. You did assume the worst, though.'

'Yes, I did.'

'They did get you to buy it, so the headlines worked.'

'Yeah, I get that.' She wrinkled her nose.

'Is it always like this? When you see stories about Henrik, do you panic like that every time?' She didn't answer.

'Do you want to get to work very badly?'

'No.'

'Let's go directly to Lysebu, then.'

'I just want to stay in the car.'

'Let's take a detour, then. If you can find one. ' Charlie took out his phone opened it, and gave it to Christine.

'There is another route, but it is very long. It will take more than twice the time.'

'Sounds perfect.' He said.

To Write a Love Song

She finally looked at Charlie. He noticed at once, and he quickly smiled back at her. She realised she had completely forgot that she was in a car with him. Maybe she had fallen asleep.

'I am sorry for being so distant,' she said. 'I guess I didn't have much sleep last night, and I'm not used to the fact that Henrik is even more known now than he ever has been before.'

'No worries, it's all very understandable. I almost threw up myself when I saw Zoey's nipples in print.' Christine laughed.

'Are you all right, though?'

'I'm getting by ... not doing great, I must admit. It's just been a hard year. Or, should I say, a hard *couple* of years.'

'Did you find him last night? You ran off like you had seen a ghost.'

'Like Cinderella?' Christine laughed at herself. *I am the reverse Cinderella, I have the prince, but it's far from a happy fairytale ending.* 'I went home. Henrik came home after a while.' Charlie steered onto a smaller road, with a slower speed. The frost crystals turned every tree into a beautiful white sculpture, and the winter sunlight made every single crystal beam.

'Is he always like that to you?' Charlie dared to ask all of a sudden. They were at an open field, and he could look at her for a few seconds without a problem.

'What do you mean?' Of course, Christine understood what he meant, but she wanted his description of last night.

'You know what I mean. Does he always forget that you're there? Does he always disappear without telling you?' Charlies voice was mild, and he tried to look at her face for a reaction.

'I know what you think. You think he was being an jerk.' Christine was calm, like it was something she was used to hear.

'Yes, I did think that. I thought he behaved like an arrogant idiot last night.' Charlie was looking at her, trying to meet her eyes.

'Understandable.' She said, while her eyes were staring out her side window. They passed a small farm with a red barn. It looked like it had just been left there to decay. But with the rays of the winter sun and the frost, it was like it was brought back to life. The red became vibrant with so much snow, and the crystals on the wood made the colour incredibly beautiful.

'He's not actually like that. Well, not all the time. Not many people know this, but Henrik is sick, you see. Well, he doesn't want to take medications for it, but his mental health is not always good. Not all the time, but sometimes it is hard to figure out whether he is sick or not, or on his way to being sick again, or if he just is like that.' Christine finally looked over towards Charlie. He kept his gaze steadily on the road. Christine sensed that he really didn't know what to say. Eventually, he looked at her.

'I know.'

'You know?' Christine stared at him and was astonished.

'I thought no one knew that.' She was afraid that this was something everyone knew, a sort of common fact among the company, and a piece of gossip that had spread around Oslo. Charlie was quiet and calm. 'Well, Harald told me, in confidence.'

It stayed quiet for a while. Then all of a sudden, Charlie continued.

'I have been involved in discussions on the prenuptial agreement for your marriage. It's all a part of what will happen to the company in the future.' Charlie kept his eyes on the road. He must have known that this would hit Christine like a bomb.

'You have *what*?' Christine started to struggle to breathe.

'Harald wants to prepare a plan for Henrik's future. If, or should I rather say "when" something happens to Harald, the whole thing will be planned. It goes into the whole process of restructuring the firm.' Charlie's gaze was still fixated on the road. Christine gave up looking into his eyes.

She took a deep breath. 'And therefore, you know all about

my life.' Christine felt a chill and put her arms around her. She wanted to be alone and tried to curl up towards the window.

'I don't know everything. I only know the information that Harald thought was necessary to set up an agreement with you. It is important for Harald that his son is in good hands after he has passed away.' Christine's hair was covering her face. She wanted to hide. Her hands were trembling. Christine tried to hide them under her armpits.

'So, what is Harald's plan for the future, then? Or is that confidential?'

'I can tell you some parts, just so you understand why I know everything a bit better, but you're a smart girl and you have probably thought about these things anyway. Harald is sixty-two and has only one child, who is not capable nor particularly interested in taking over after him. He is also wondering if Henrik is able to take care of himself at times. It's all too much for one person to inherit and have control over anyway, particularly Henrik. Especially if he is in a manic period.'

'I sort of knew that,' Christine replied, 'but what will happen?'

'That's one of the reasons he hired me. Harald trusts you like no-one else. The firm will have an overall plan which we are working on, but he needs you to have some control over Henrik's shares when Harald passes, with a board of course.'

'That's why I accepted to work for Harald in the first place. I was doing quite well by myself. I felt it was the right thing to do, a way of taking care of Henrik, you know, to ease the pressure off him. To let him be free to do what he dreams of doing. So what is the essence of the deal then?'

'He wants you to be Henriks guardian if you get married or not.'

'We have always planned to get married, even though we are not engaged yet, so you can say "when", and not "if." Christine knew at the moment she said it, that it maybe wouldn't happen.

'All right, then,' Charlie said carefully. 'The deal mostly gives you control over Henrik's personal economy and shares. You will take his seat at the board of the holding company. You will get some shares as well if, I am sorry, *when* you marry. If you divorce, you can continue to be the his guardian if you wish. Harald and Wenche know that you will always look after Henrik, no matter how he behaves. If you at some point don't want the guardian role, you have to find a suitable replacement.'

Christine felt intimidated. There was a feeling of sadness, and of responsibility. She had always felt emotionally responsible for

Henrik, but never for his finances, but she knew that Harald had more control over his personal spending than you would think. This was the financial control over Henrik from Harald to her.

'We've just tried to map out all the future possibilities. It is Harald and Wenches' choice to sort this out now. It is a part of structuring the company and preparing it for when Harald isn't there. Henrik's health and career is a key part. The diagnosis of the disease that makes it even more obvious he is not suitable.' Christine took a deep breath. *Am I the only one that haven't given up on Henrik? The only one who waits for him to come home and stay here with me, and live a normal life?* She said nothing, but she felt a chill down her back. *It's as if everyone is planning our future, except Henrik and I.*

'We have not been planning your life,' he said. Like he was reading her mind. 'You and Henrik, of course, make the life choices for you yourself. I have just been part of the planning of what happens with the shares.' He looked at her. She was hiding her face in her hands, and her head was bowed down. She had kicked off her shoes and had her feet up on the seat, with her knees under her chin.

'You are signing up for a good life no matter what state Henrik's health is in.'

'Am I really, though?' Christine said in a sad, desperate voice.

Charlie looked at her again, and seemed to know what she meant.

'Well, a good life financially, but it also comes with responsibility for Henrik and Henrik's future children, wether they are illegitimate or not.'

'Thanks. That's enough!' She said aggressively and started shouting 'I do not want to know about the rights of Henrik's future or, for all I know, PRESENT illigitimate children! I never asked for this information!'

Charlie took a deep breath and continued. 'Harald wanted me to prepare you for the possibility of this agreement. I see that after the headlines today, this maybe wasn't the best day. Harald and Wenche care as much about you as they do about Henrik. They know that your life with Henrik will never be easy, they know he what he appears to be. They know his heath is a permanent challenge, and Harald and Wenche are worried.'

Christine didn't say anything.

'All in all, I know Henrik has his challenged. I thought you should know that. It felt strange lying about that to you. I hope you can keep this to yourself, but if you would rather talk to Harald about this, he wouldn't mind. He knows of course that I am telling you this.'

Christine didn't open her mouth for a while. Charlie probably realised he had said enough and kept driving.

'And what do you know about me, then?' Christine asked after a time. Charlie looked at her quickly. She had lifted her face from her palms and looked at him.

'Just what is necessary to know to set up a good agreement. In addition to whatever Harald tells me.'

'So what do you know then, about me?' Christine kept her gaze on him, trying to figure out whether he was hiding something or not. Charlie smiled. 'I can tell that Harald and Wenche adore you. I believe they have used the words incredible, amazing, genuine, kind, clever, trustworthy, and grounded. You have never taken advantage of the connections you have through them, you avoid attention. Basically they couldn't dream of anyone better.'

'Wow,' was all she managed to say. Christine felt a bit uncomfortable hearing all the nice things about her. She knew it was Harald and Wenche who had said those things, but it felt like Charlie meant them as well. Charlie looked quickly at her.

'Harald is worried about your life with Henrik, that's all.'

Christine knew Harald was right to worry, it was just so heartbreaking to hear that it was obvious to Harald as well.

'And you now agree with him? After last night?' Christine

said in a low voice, looking out the window.

'I don't know your relationship. No one really does but you. I have to admit that Henrik's behaviour last night wasn't great. I assume Harald has seen that behaviour before.'

Christine knew the relationship was not perfect, and in a phase where it felt almost non-existent. 'This is creeping me out. You know so much about me, and I have met you like what, two times? Three times?'

'I know it's tough to hear. I just thought it was better to tell you know, before … '

'Before what? I got married? We become friends?' Christine felt overwhelmed, and angry. She felt like throwing up again.

'I am trying to relate to this professionally, as Harald's employee and adviser. I must take Harald's concerns seriously. I think you should at least know my role. It felt a bit weird knowing so much about you, and not tell you.'

Christine had to think before she answered. 'It's just so weird to have someone that is so honest with me, and who know so much about me. It feels very intimidating; I feel exposed. I want to hide under a duvet, and just stay there and not come out for a very long time.'

'That's quite understandable, but it's just me and two lawyers, not the world.' Charlie tried to give her a comforting smile, which helped.

*

The road was going into a forest, and Charlie had to slow down.

'Maybe you should get to know me better then. So it doesn't feel so intrusive that I know that much about you, and not vice versa.'

Christine looked at him and smiled. 'Really?'

'Go on then, ask me anything, maybe it will make you feel a little bit better.'

Christine turned around in her seat, so she was facing Charlie. She still had her feet in the seat, now crossed legged. 'You promise you will tell the truth?'

'Promise.' Charlie smiled quickly at her.

"What is your worst habit?" Christine was enjoying this.

'Eating a cinnamon bun as breakfast every day. I had chocolate for a long time, but a cinnamon bun must be healthier.'

'Is it really? That's a poor excuse for eating a cinnamon bun each morning!' Christine was laughing.

'What's your guilty pleasure then?'

'Ahh … It's difficult to pick one. I must say cars, I love old cars. Maybe one day I'll have a big garage with cars I can only drive for two months each year. And I'll go on road trips with a weekend bag and sleep at fancy inns. Like retired people. Only I want to do it now.'

'That's not a proper guilty pleasure. It's more like a strong interest or hobby. It's not embarrassing at all. Let's try something else. Ever hit someone?'

'Yes.. once.'

' I didn't think you were the type.'

'Neither did I. I was quite surprised I did that. A guy gave my little sister a lot of alcohol, I assume he had other intentions. She is four years younger than me, and she was 14 at the time. I have always been very protective of her - I still am. She wouldn't be allowed to do anything if it was up to me. And I still don't like that she drinks.'

'She might do worse things than drinking…' She waggled her eyebrows suggestingly.

'Shut up.'

'So … When did you lose your virginity?' Christine had a

huge grin, and a mischievous look.

'Oh, low blow …'

'You promised.'

'That smile is worth the embarrassing questions. Okay. I was actually twenty. It wasn't until my second year at university. In my defence I went to an all-boys school, and that left me with a massive handicap. I had no idea how to talk to girls, and I had no clue what to do when I liked someone.'

"So how many girls have you managed to sleep with since then?'

'You are really taking advantage of this situation". He smiled flirtatiously at her. 'Since you have been with Henrik since you were sixteen, and I can therefore assume your number.'

'That is sadly correct. Only one, yes. And I was 16 by the way.'

'Well since you beat me at age, at least I will beat you at numbers. I am not so embarrassed to say this, but maybe I should be. I have to count one extra time, maybe it will be higher.'

'Done yet?'

'Yes. It's only five.'

"Hmm, that sounds honest at least. But yeah, maybe a bit

low?'

'Shut up. I've worked a lot, and I am terrible at flirting. I have managed to date three of them over a longer period of time. I would actually say it's pretty impressive, considering how hopeless I am.'

'Have you ever been in love, then?'

'Yes. I thought I was at least, but not with any of those five.'

'When and with who?'

'When I was nineteen, and her name was Fiona. I had classes with her at university.'

'What happened?'

'Absolutely nothing. She broke my heart without knowing. She got together with Ben. Or he slept with her for a while. Treated her quite badly I would say - he wasn't in love with her. But he thought she was hot, and that was reason enough for Ben. He has always been the confident type, so it was no problem for him. I was absolutely heartbroken for at least a year. I even wrote a song about her on the piano in the common room at our halls, but I never sang the lyrics out loud. I just sang them in my head.'

'Ahhhhh …' Christine tilted her head. 'That's so sweet, you have written a love song? You're quite the romantic then! Have you written more love songs?'

'No, it was just silly. It must have been hormones from my teenage years that had just been bottled up. You know, so many years without girls.'

'Think you'll write one again one day?'

'Absolutely not. I think I just really wanted to feel like what it was to have a girlfriend, and I ended up knowing what heartbreak was instead.'

'Have you been jealous again, then?'

'I can't tell you,' Charlie smiled secretly. Christine touched his shoulder.

'You're not allowed to have any secrets. Since I don't get to have any.'

'The fact that I know some things about your relationship is not the same as not having secrets from me. Secrets are the things that are just in your head, that media can't figure out, and things no one but you know. I think you have a lot of secrets. Dreams, thoughts, doubts and hopes. Just like anyone else. What about you then? Ever been jealous?'

'Yes, envious at least, sometimes at Heidi. It would just be nice once in a while to be as confident and carefree as she is.

Boys just swoon over her. It would just be nice, though, to sometimes get the attention she gets. Being in a relationship for so many years when everyone else just flirts around do sometimes feel a bit lonely.'

'Isn't being lonely what being in a relationship should be the opposite of?'

'I guess so. I have been speared from the heartbreak at least. Or at least the proper heartbreak. I guess earlier today might have been a preview.'

Charlie said nothing. Christine just sighed and looked out the window. Christine watched the snow which covered the world with a calm and beautiful blanket pass by them.

'I can recommend writing a lovesong.' He suddenly said jestingly.

Christine and burst out laughing.

The Manhood Test

Christine must have fallen asleep again, because all of a

sudden, they were in a completely different place, along a lake.

'It's so amazing how the snow makes everything quieter. Not just the sound, but it feels like the snow lowers my pulse. Everything that I might be stressed about is not so important when I look at a snow-covered landscape,' Christine said in a low voice, mostly to herself.

'How are you feeling, then? Has the drive calmed you a bit?' Charlie asked.

'I think so.'

'Are you prepared for the media tonight, then?'

'I am never ready for them.'

'Do you want to avoid them? We could make sure you get a room in the main building, so you don't have to pass them to get to dinner.'

'I think I'll be fine - have you been to the ski jump, Charlie?'

'I have only seen it from a far. It looks pretty silly.'

'Do you want to stop by? The view is amazing, and it must be looking its best today.'

'Since I have been so honest, there's no point in stopping now. I am afraid of heights. Actually, that was an understatement. I am *terrified* of heights, and I start to sweat and shiver.'

'I'll hold your hand. It's not dangerous at all. We're not the ones who are going to jump. There's an elevator up there so you don't have to climb stairs with shaking legs.'

'I don't really want to go on a ski lift.'

'Don't worry, it's an actual elevator, like inside a building.'

'I'm still not sure.'

'Please! Do it for me. I need to feel the air, and the freedom.'

'All right, but I have to warn you, I will get mad.'

'You will get mad?'

'Yes, I get very angry when I'm scared. I get mad for putting myself at risk. I will get mad if you look over the rail, because I will think it is a very stupid thing to do, and I will be afraid something might happen. I will also get angry with you for dragging me up there in the first place. Just so you know, and I apologise in advance.'

'Apology accepted in advance. Will you be angry with me afterwards as well?'

'I might be. It depends on how terrifying the experience is.'

'Ok, I'll take the chance,' Christine grinned.

'I might never speak to you again.' Charlie looked seriously at her.

She paused and looked at him. Then she started smiling. 'I think I'm willing to risk it.'

*

Charlie had barely managed to park the car before Christine jumped out.

'Come on! It will be great! There is not a cloud in sight, no wind at all, and not a single tourist bus here. If we hurry, we can see the sunset!'

He smiled and walked slowly after her.

'So, people actually put skis on, and set off? They must have some sort of brain defect.' he said. Christine smiled at his attempt to sound rational.

'Henrik has actually jumped from here.' She laughed.

'Of course he has.' Charlie said mumbled.

'I didn't say that to make you feel bad, just to agree on your point that there might indeed be a brain defect.'

'Is it some sort of ritual that all Nordic men must do?' Charlie looked up to the sky.

'Ha ha! That would be a quick way of wiping out all Norwegian men. No… You have to do it as a sport, and practice for a long time on smaller jumps. Eventually, you will be allowed to jump this one.'

'Henrik is pretty crazy. But I guess those ski films are less controlled and more dangerous than this thing.'

'That's true. I guess I have been with him for so long I forgot that this ski jump is also pretty dangerous.'

'This is embarrassing for me. Here you are, like a five-year-old at Christmas, your boyfriend has jumped off this thing and I am shaking already.' Charlies was clinging on to a handrail which was supposed to manage the line of visitors.

'We all have our fears, we just have different ones. I was sick earlier today, that was quite embarrassing as well.' Christine gave him a comforting smile.

'Promise me you will be next to me the whole time we're up there.' He looked terrified, his brows where far up on his forehead.

'I promise. You can hold my hand whenever you need.'

They didn't speak in the elevator. Christine was smiling with excitement, while Charlie looked nervous. As the doors opened, she said, 'If you are so scared, why are you doing this?'

'I just don't want this time with you to end.' He looked her in the eyes. She was quite surprised by his frankness. She felt the temperature rising in her cheeks, and she was hoping he wouldn't notice that she was blushing. *How does Heidi deal with these things all the time?* She smiled shyly, and quickly turned her head and looked at the view instead. *Am I leading him on? Am I flirting with him?* She walked out to the middle of the deck, and he followed her.

The sun was just setting, almost disappearing behind a blue mountain far away. There was some fog that was lying at the bottom of the fjord, which extinguished the notion of land and sea. The sky was bleeding red to the west, and to the east, it was already the most beautiful deep blue, which would soon cover the whole sky.

'I know everyone loves sunsets, but I love the blue hour,' began Christine. 'It's not as extravagant and intense as a sunset can be, but it has this beautiful, calm atmosphere, where everything is resting, like the pulse of the day has decreased, and everything is calm. Every corner of the city becomes beautiful in the blue hour. The lights become so warm, and the rest so cold. It's like the quiet nightcap after a great party. You know, when you've gotten home, and you put on just a single light. You kick off your shoes, take off your earrings that were too heavy, and you just sit there on your sofa in a beautiful gown, with an old classic jazz record playing. You do prefer the song on a live piano, but a record will do. Completely comfortable, and you feel great. That's what the blue hour is to me. The sunset is the party, with so much going on, and the blue hour is the quiet contrast.' She could see that he was starting to relax a bit from her words.

As they stood there, the lights from all around the fjord started to appear. They became small diamonds in a dark sea.

'This is unbelievably magical. I had no idea that the snow and frost would make an even greater sunset.' Charlie was standing there completely startled.

'Are you just a tiny bit glad I dragged you up here?' Christine started to move closer to the railings.

'I am both terrified and excited at the same time. I've heard that the greatest experiences in life are like this.'

'Oh yeah? Which ones?'

'Well, you could start with the physical stuff, like flying, climbing, and then there's the emotional stuff, like falling in love, and having a child - but I guess that is both physical and emotional. We shouldn't *not* do things just because they scare us.

We might miss out on a great experience.'

'Well, this makes me feel free, at least. It's just the rest of the world that sometimes terrifies me.' Christine stepped closer to the railings again. She was wondering when Charlie would stop her. The closer she got to the edge, the more in control she felt. She felt free, everything else didn't mean anything. Up here she could control her emotions, could handle herself. She thought to herself that she should remember this feeling when she didn't feel good enough, and she felt the world was against her.

These last twenty-four hours had been horrible, not because they really *were*, but because she had let the world get to her. She promised herself that she would never let anything get to her again: not any newspapers, not any rumours, not Henrik. She promised herself that she would never let her own insecurities take over her mind like that again. She walked all out to the corner of the deck. Whenever she had a great height under her, Christine could feel her knees tingling. Right now, she felt invincible.

'Can you please get back here, to the middle? Please! You promised me. Don't lean against the balustrade, at least!' Charlie's voice was desperate, his fear evident in the short breaths he took between almost each word.

'Are you really that scared? It's not something you just say?'

Christine had turned around but was still at the corner.

'Can't you just get to the middle again?'

'Sure.'

As she got closer, she reached for Charlie's hand, although he was still in the middle of the deck. He looked surprised at it. She smiled comfortably at him and he put his hand in hers. She dragged him slowly closer to the railings. He was trembling, likely from the cold and from the fear at the same time.

'I can't believe I let you do this to me.'

'It's easier when you're with me, right? It is pretty great to see the view below as well, isn't it?' She faced him the whole time. 'Just trust me, and don't forget to take deep breaths.' She stopped quite close to the edge. Charlie was concentrating on breathing. Then all of a sudden, he seemed to realised that it was ok. He started to smile, and then he started to laugh.

'We should go back, so you don't freeze to death,' Christine said.

'Yes, it's absolutely freezing. Now that I am here, I don't really want to go, though.'

Christine knew that he was talking about holding her hand, and not leaving the view.

'We have to go back, though.'

When they got to the stairs, she let go of his hand. In the elevator, they didn't speak. She looked at him, and then she quickly looked away. When they got to the car, still not a word was spoken. Christine didn't know whether it was awkward silence after they had been holding hands, or wether they where both relaxed.

*

They drove further uphill and reached Lysebu within a few minutes. They both got out of the car, and he took out her luggage for her.

'Thanks for the ride, and everything,' Christine finally said.

'The pleasure was all mine. Thank you for a great day! Or for me at least, your day must very understandably have been pretty tough. But there also wasn't anything that bad in the media. Don't let that Zoey girl get to you. And also, you were definitely the best-dressed last night.'

Christine didn't say anything, she just smiled.

'The media will be here tonight as well though,' Charlie said carefully.

'I know. I think I will be okay.'

*

Christine unlocked the door to her room. She had gotten a room in an older building, opposite the main building. The hotel consisted of buildings that looked like to have all been a part of an old farm, with all buildings transformed to function as a small, boutique hotel. She was entering a cosy, old mountain cabin in solid timber, and she could smell the wood. The key was solid iron with a long tassel attached.

Christine felt relaxed as she entered the room. There was something about these old buildings that made one forget about once own life, even though just for a few seconds. The cabin was probably used as sleeping facility a long time ago, since it had an old stove in the corner. The bed looked particularly tempting. She sat down on it with all her clothes on and let her head fall backwards onto the pillow. She couldn't wait until the evening was over so she could sleep as long as she wanted.

*

She tried to call Henrik. There was no reply. It was actually what she had wished for.

Flirting with an Employee

Christine took a look at herself in the mirror. She was tired, the bags under her eyes where darker than usual, but not as bad as expected. The makeup had helped a lot, as well as an hour of sleep. The dress she wore was maybe a bit loose; she probably should have had it fitted, but she had never felt comfortable in clothing that was too tight. She wrapped her fur cape over her shoulders for the short walk across the courtyard. Then she put on her earrings; although they were not too big, since they were the real deal, they were so heavy. Christine was wondering for how long she would have them on, but she knew she couldn't leave them anywhere. She took a deep breath and grabbed the doorknob. It was still freezing outside, and her breath turned to vapour at once. She looked over to the main entrance, where she saw the photographers was set up, and started to walk towards it. She had her shoes in a shoe bag underneath her cape, and flat boots under her dress, so she didn't slip. Leather soles on hard snow was a very bad idea, and she felt pretty smart hiding her shoes under her cape. Christine knew that showing up solo would get her more attention, but she felt she had no other choice. She was ready to show the press that the headlines earlier didn't bother her at all.

'You look great tonight!' A photographer shouted to her to get her attention.

However, Christine had decided to not answer any question; it could be a slippery slope. She just smiled, as if everything was okay. *Which it is, or isn't it? Well, if I don't know, they don't know.*

'Are you alone tonight? Are you okay with Henrik's so-called friendship with Zoey? When are you moving to London? Are you and Henrik still together after last night?' She managed to just smile. Wenche and Harald was standing at the entrance. Once she was next to them, Wenche through her arms around Christine's neck, to show the press that everything was alright.

'They are terribly interested in you, but we hope it doesn't bother you too much.'

'It's okay,' Christine replied politely, and then entered the hall. It wasn't the media that was a problem, the problem was that she didn't know if she trusted Henrik. She felt it was the one thing Harald and Wenche couldn't do anything about, and it didn't help to complain about it. In the reception area Christine accepted a glass of champagne. She was so comfortable this year compared to last year.

*

She looked at her seating plan on her way in. In contrast to last year, she was more fortunate with her dining partner. She was next to Kristian Bang, a very charming and well-behaved family friend, who Christine had met a couple of times before. Charlie was also at the table, and by his side was Heidi. She had, without a doubt, been upgraded from last year. Christine all of a sudden remembered that she hadn't spoken to Heidi and felt bad because she hadn't told her friend that she would be at the office foyer for drinks. Christine wanted to find Heidi straight away. As she looked around the room, she immediately spotted Charlie. As if he had some kind of radar, he looked at her at the same moment. He gave her a polite nod, as if he was bowing in secret, and smiled. Christine shyly smiled back, but quickly started to look for Heidi instead. She found some colleagues, and walked over to them to see if they had arrived with Heidi. Christine noticed that Charlie was still looking at her, probably baffled by her cold rejection.

*

Christine didn't find Heidi before it was time to find her seat. She saw that her seat was close to the big windows, and thought she might head back to the cloakroom to grab her fur cape in case there was a chill from the windows. The cloakroom attendant wasn't there. She snuck into the wardrobe, which was now filled with coats and furs. She found her cape and stretched her hand into the shoe bag to find her shawl. All of a sudden, she felt someone was beside her, and before she could explain herself, she saw that it was Charlie. He leaned in and whispered to her:

'At least I got you at my table. Maybe I get a dance later?

Your dance card can't be full yet, is it?' Christine took a step back, and if there was was room for more, she would have taken two. There was only one way out, and Charlie was blocking that way.

'My future in-laws, my boss, and *your* boss are arranging this dinner,' she whispered back. 'It is a work event. All of my colleagues, and people I do not trust, are here. Everyone will be watching tonight. Thank you for your support earlier, I needed something else to think about, which was nice. But the day is over now.' Christine was cold and quiet at the same time and passed Charlie quickly to get into the hallway. He gave her a concerned gaze, like he was looking for a heart in her eyes. She felt like she had trodden on him with one of her high heels. Maybe she had been a bit brutal. As she stepped into the hallway, she saw Alex at the other end. She was startled, and Alex must have sensed it, as he gave off a suspicious look with his eyebrows. She was still afraid that Charlie would grab her from behind. She tried to walk quickly, but not in a way that would show she was stressed, and gave Alex a polite smile as she passed him.

'How do you do, Alex?' she said, a bit too loudly, hoping Charlie would take the hint.

'Looking good, Chrissy.. you better hurry, I think Harald is about to start. I thought I should take a piss before, as he likes his own voice a bit too well to last a pint." Alex was sleazy as always.

Christine was hoping Charlie wouldn't exit the wardrobe before Alex had passed, but she didn't dare to turn around. Her heart sank when she heard his footsteps as well.

*

She was quickly back at her place at the table. Since everyone in the room was standing, she was not too late. She smiled at Kristian, and gave him a kiss on both cheeks. She greeted the rest of the table. She quickly greeted Heidi across the room, knowing they would catch up later. Christine was so relieved to have Kristian by her side. He was sweet, chatty, but most of all, married to Harald's best friend's daughter. In a way, he was in the same position as Christine: married into a very rich family. His wife, Nanna, was very pleasant and beautiful, and they seemed like a perfect couple, with two perfect kids. Nanna's family was not so perfect on the other hand; her dad was a notorious cheater, and married for the fourth time. Harald was a better father-in-law, Christine thought, but the rest, she was maybe jealous of. Nanna was known for being very down to earth, never on a spending too much, and being a devoted mother and wife, always at home. It seemed like she just wanted a regular life.

Christine noticed that Charlie was behind his chair as well, but he didn't look at her. *I was maybe a bit harsh with him in the cloakroom, but what were we doing earlier? I held his hand. That can't be normal friend behaviour, he must understand that it was a mistake.* She was shocked with herself. Even if Henrik wasn't there at the moment, she felt that she was back in reality. It was a strange thing to say about a white-tie gala, but it felt more real than earlier. She was with Henrik, and a part of his family.

Kristian started to speak about he found it weird at first to be in Nanna's life, but after a while he was comfortable with it, and knew he was the ingredient of normal that she needed in her life.

'You know, I didn't grow up with Nanna like you did with Henrik,' he said.

'That doesn't mean I am used to it though,' Christine laughed.

'You have to think of the two of you as a team; a team in his family things, and in your family.'

'I think we are more player and manager. There are a few things I don't think I will ever get used to.'

'I feel the same. But we should write an instruction manual, or a memo. You know, to the poor guys that will marry our children. A "dos and don'ts" sort of thing.'

The lady at the other side of Kristian said something to him, and all of a sudden, she didn't have Kristian's full attention. She looked over at Charlie again. He was whispering something to Heidi, his head unusually close for a regular conversation. Christine pretended to take part in Kristian's conversation, but she was really just observing Heidi and Charlie. Heidi had put her flirting in a high gear. Christine knew all the signs. She was tossing her hair, she was laughing at everything he said. She was laughing so much, guests at other tables were turning around to see what was going on at their table. *Is Charlie really that funny?* Christine didn't find him that funny at all, and now Heidi was about to fall off her chair. Charlie seemed to love the attention he got from Heidi, he was leaning towards her, looking at her all the time, completely forgetting the others at the table. How could she have let herself be charmed by Charlie earlier today? Christine felt that she had been very wrong about him. She had seen a vulnerable and sweet Charlie today, and now he was a total player. *He is obviously a big flirt, how could I have fallen for that earlier today?* Christine felt that she had let Heidi down. Not only had she forgotten her earlier, but she had held hands with the guy Heidi was very obviously keen on dating, which was not okay. Not just because she herself was with Henrik, but because her best friend was clearly falling for him. He now had his arm at the back of her chair. A small bell rang. Christine knew that it was time for the annual welcome speech from Harald. Heidi and Charlie continued without noticing the bell. Finally, the man next to Heidi had to interrupt them and tell them to be quiet. At that point, Harald was already speaking. That was when Charlie finally looked at Christine. It was an intense unpleasant look. *As if he knew I would be watching him.* Christine turned away quickly and looked at Harald instead, and did not look in Charlie's direction again. She kept her gaze on Harald, but she couldn't focus on what he said.

'Company changing … How would this happen? My son, who I am very proud of … success in other arenas … Charlie is therefore taking over as CEO of the whole company, as we have found him best-suited to lead all the different branches of the company.'

Harald said what? Charlie was the new CEO for the whole company? Christine didn't know *exactly* what it meant, but she knew that Charlie was in complete control of Henrik already, and by extension her. He would be her boss during the day as well. She looked down at the table and tried to avoid Charlie at all costs. She understood that Charlie was an extremely well-paid man now, and that he would have women throwing themselves at his feet. *Just like Henrik.* What had she managed to get herself tangled up in? She knew she might be exaggerating the problem at bit, but she knew that holding his hand today was a big mistake. She shouldn't be charmed by him, he was not as innocent as he seemed earlier. She shouldn't even be *friends* with him. *I should be loyal to Henrik, the love of my life. Henrik is just in a phase.* She saw out of the corner of her eye that Charlie was looking at her, probably to watch her reaction. She tried to think about her good memories with Henrik, but it didn't work, her guilt just started again. It was just chaos with Henrik, and she didn't know what to think. Now Charlie stood up, about to say some things himself. Christine tried to look out the big windows because she knew the view was amazing, although it was pitch black now. She thought about the long cross-country skiing trips she had had by herself and with her dad through the forest below. It worked.

*

All of a sudden, Christine heard applause, and she knew the speech was over. Charlie went to his table again, and Christine was speaking to Kristian already, and barely noticed Charlie out of the corner of her eye. After a string of courses, cheeses, desserts and a whole lot of ignoring the other side of the table, Kristian asked for a dance. Christine was so relieved to leave the table.

'Come on, the band has everything! How many brass instruments can you even count in there?' Christine grabbed Kristian's hand, while the band was already playing a classic song.

'What do you know?' He asked.

'As in dances? I only know the swing and waltz. Are there more I should know? Is that a chapter in the wealthy family instructions that I have missed? Should I know the foxtrot?'

'Nah, I actually did ballroom dancing when I was younger,' explained Kristian. My mother was teaching, and instead of getting a babysitter, I had to join in. My wife has absolutely no rhythm whatsoever, so I enjoy dancing with anyone else, really. Just let me lead, and you'll be okay.' Kristian was an amazing dancer, and managed to make Christine feel like a star. She had danced *pas de deux* as a ballet dancer, which she had never enjoyed since she was so tall, and dancing with Henrik was fun, but he was all over the place, and it was mostly about him. Dancing with Kristian was completely different. As she was twirling around, Christine had noticed that people were looking at them. She had also spotted Charlie at the bar, with Heidi. It annoyed her that she always knew where he was. After a while she managed to tell him that she probably had to mingle, since she felt she was partly hosting in the absence of Henrik.

'Let me know if you want another go,' Kristian said.

'Why don't you give your wife a spin? No one can dance to this song anyway.' Christine was backing away from him.

'I promised her after our wedding that I would never drag her out here again. Not even a slow waltz could cover that horror show.'

Christine was relieved that Nanna wasn't perfect, although it was still a charming flaw. Christine went straight into the bar area, knowing it was time for her to mingle with all the guests. It was as she had told Charlie earlier a work event, and she knew she had to keep that in mind for the rest of the night. She was good at it, almost like she was Henrik that night. *Quite different from last year.*

*

The hours passed by, but she always took notice of where Charlie was. At the end of the night, when most guests had left, she knew she was almost next to him. Alex was all of a sudden a few feet away from her, and Christine knew she had to be polite - and, at the same time, continue to avoid Charlie.

'So, where's Henrik tonight?' Alex was not known for being tactful.

'He's still in London. Only I travelled back to be here. Henrik was never meant to be here. He's not at the seating plan.' Christine knew they had learned from last year and had a cover name for his seat instead, so there wouldn't be an embarrassing incident if he didn't show up.

'So you're covering his ass then?'

'Not really, he doesn't need to be here. I am more active in the firm, so I should be here.'

'You're covering his ass all the time, then. A prettier and a better replacement, I mean, at least you're more qualified than Henrik.'

'I didn't have to take this job. I had another job before this that was quite okay, and you know that.' Christine's response was sharp and loud.

'Yeah, I know, but wasn't that job also because of Harald?' Alex was smug and calm. 'But how bad can you actually screw up? It's not like Harald has given you freedom to buy stocks by yourself, he always double check your advise, don't ?'

Before Christine could say anything, Charlie was by her side. He but obviously understood that Christine was offended and uncomfortable.

'Evening, Alex,' Charlie said in a sharp voice.

'Hi, Charlie. Christine and I were just talking about her luck, you know, with getting that position at your office.'

'Well, she was more than qualified. We're honoured that

someone with her resume and accomplishments wanted to work for us.'

'Come on. If it wasn't for the fact that she was dating Henrik, she would have been the first to go if you could use the axe as you wanted to.'

'As interesting it is for me to hear how I should lead the company, I must inform you that I have looked over the resumes of all employees in our top positions, and I have to disappoint you on that regard. Miss Loveness' resume is one of the most impressive. I am sure we wouldn't have managed to persuade her to work for us if it wasn't for the family relation, so we are, despite your concerns, more than pleased she is also a part of the family.'

Alex mumbled something about Christine's tits and walked away.

'Are you all right?' Charlie turned to her.

'Thank you. That was very nice of you, but not necessary. I am used to that stuff, sadly - especially from him.'

'I defend all of my employees. Don't read anything else into it.' Charlie was clearly trying to be casual and cool.

'Don't worry, I know you treat all your female employees

with great attention,' Christine snapped back.

'Well, at least I don't spend my nights having a dance performance at work events.' Charlie turned around and leaned against the bar.

'Flirting with an employee is not very professional either, at least I'm not the boss of the firm.' Christine leaned against the bar as well, trying to keep her calm.

'Your flirting with a married man, when your absent boyfriends family is hosting. That won't help the rumour mill, now will it?'

Christine could feel his words in her stomach.

'It was friendly and innocent, while your flirt on the other hand is head-over-heels for you. At least I'm not playing with the emotions of an employee, a receptionist to be precise. Could it be more cliché and inappropriate?"

Charlie just gave Christine a stare.

"Look, she's coming over, so don't let me ruin your luck tonight. Heidi is all yours. You know, you pretend to be terrible with girls, but that's how you play them, right? Heidi shouldn't be too difficult to persuade.'

'That's not a very nice thing to say about your best friend.

Says a lot about you, really.'

'You're her boss.' Christine faked a smile as Heidi came near.

'Christine, I haven't spoken to you all night! How was the premiere? I saw the pictures You looked amazing!'

'Thanks, sweetie. It probably looked fancier than it was, but Henrik was relieved. I would rather spend an evening with good friends than in a room full of strangers. It was pretty boring, actually.'

Charlie gave Christine a disappointing look.

'So,.' Christine started. 'I think the two of you have to continue the night without me. I'm sure you won't mind if I call it a night. I'll call you tomorrow, Heidi.'

'Christine!' Heidi shouted after her. 'Don't leave!' Christine turned around and smiled at her. Once she got to the door, she turned around again. She noticed that Charlie was still looking at her, but quickly looked away.

Wet Feet in Boots

As she laid there with her head on her pillow, Christine's thoughts wouldn't let her sleep. She was sure Heidi liked Charlie a lot, so it was right of her to go to bed. *Why do I care so much that Heidi likes Charlie? Why can I just let it go?* Christine remembered that she should try to call Henrik, although it was almost two o'clock. Maybe it would help to hear his voice.

*

There was no answer. It was nice to hear his voicemail message at least. She rang several times, just to hear his voice. It calmed her.

*

Christine tossed and turned. Had she been asleep? She turned her duvet around. She tried to lie at the other end of the bed. She sat for a while. She checked her phone, although she had the sound on. She pulled the curtains back a bit and looked out the window. She wondered if the pool was still open; maybe that would help her sleep afterwards. Christine found her swimsuit that was always in her luggage. She took a peek outside again. It seemed like the party was over. She put on her swimsuit, her bathrobe, her fur cape over that, and her boots. Enough layers for the run across the courtyard. She laughed at herself when she passed the mirror by the door. *This is so strange it could be a in a fashion magazine.* Christine brought her big key with her and started her run to the main building. As she entered the main door, she could see a few guests still in the bar. She could hear them, but luckily, they couldn't see her.

*

She managed to reach the pool doors without meeting anyone, and she hoped there weren't anyone who thought it was a good idea to continue the party in the pool or hot tub. When she opened the door, Christine saw some empty glasses, but no one was there. It was quiet, and the big windows were covered in condensation because of the cold outside. The light from the pool room lit up the first few meters of snow outside. She took off her boots by the door and hung up her cape and bathrobe. She tried to dive in as smooth as possible, then took long, slow strokes. Christine liked to be underwater. It was so nice to be in a different element. She loved the stillness of the sounds. She tried to just go above for air.

*

Suddenly she noticed a shadow above her, standing at the side of the pool. Someone had been in the sauna. As she went up for air, Christine lifted her head towards the window and saw Charlie's image reflected in the glass. She took a deep breath and went underwater again. She just wanted to be alone, but eventually Christine had to go above water again. Charlie had sat down at the edge and had put his feet into the pool. He had pulled up his bathrobe, so high that she was wondering if he was wearing swimming shorts under there or not.

'Hi,' she said when she reached the end of the pool, and turned around.

'Hi,' he replied without looking back at her. She started to swim again, this time above water. As she passed him, he asked, 'have I done something to you?'

'Not really.'

'Then why won't you speak to me?'

'I am speaking to you.'

Charlie took a deep breath: 'Can you stop, please?'

'I couldn't sleep. I thought this would wear me out.'

'What kept you awake?'

'The comment from Alex, mostly.' Christine knew she was lying. 'I guess I just have to get used to it. '

"Look, there will always be people who are jealous, and they will always find reasons why you have succeeded, and they have not. Don't you think I haven't heard that as well? Don't let it get to you.'

'I just feel that being a part of that family is all I am. I have joined a great team, and I need to be satisfied with just being a part of it.'

'You should try not to let it overshadow your own self worth. You should try and always follow your instincts and passions, not a duty.'

'I stopped following my own passions and wants years ago. I could never just follow my dream, that would be silly.' Christine liked having these conversations with Charlie. She had almost forgotten the previous hours.

'What was your passion then?' Charlie was smiling.

'I'm not going to tell you, it is embarrassing. "An unreachable dream" would be an understatement.'

'Come on, tell me. You're not the type that would dream of being a "pop star" or something like that.' The tone was back to what it was earlier that day, with the same flirtatious smile hidden in every word he said.

'It was "ballet". But I was too tall, so it would have been a very short career. I danced a lot, even though I knew it wasn't a career option. I quit when I started university in Bergen, to focus on my studies. But, if I could choose in life, without a concern, I would just dance. I loved it, I loved everything about it. Getting up early to get to a class before school, the repetitive barre stretching, the pain of toes on point. Being the last one to leave the studio at night. I liked being there alone, just me and the music. I don't need an audience.'

'So you miss it?'

'I guess so, but, I go to the ballet in Oslo, so I get to see a lot.' Christine had stopped swimming and was beside Charlie. She was resting on the edge of the pool, while he was still sitting. She pulled herself up from the water and turned so she sat next to him. Charlie grabbed a towel from a shelf behind him and put it over her shoulders.

'Thank you.' Christine now dared to meet his eyes. The room was hot, and the condensation on the windows made it almost impossible to see outside.

'What about you? Are you living your dream? You're the new CEO of billion-dollar empire. And you're how old? Thirty-four? That's insane. There are articles about you in newspapers and magazines. On top of everything, you have gotten where you are by yourself. You are an annoying over-achiever.'

'It's not my goal, you know. It is not what I want to do for the rest of my life, but I did find this job a great challenge for a few years. The thing is, I don't do it for anyone else than me, and that frees me. I can quit any day because I don't feel like I am doing it for anyone. If I have to give something up that I care about to have this job, I will quit, without hesitation. I think people that do endless things for other people and never get anything in return are more over-achievers than me. Because they feel like they should. Not because it's what they really want to do."

'You might be saying that, but I don't believe you. You wouldn't quit any day.'

'Sure, I would. The opportunity is great, but there will be other opportunities as well. The salary and bonuses should never be the sole reason for staying.'

'Are you considering not saying yes to the job?'

'I have said yes to the position, but I might not have it for a great length of time. It depends on what happens. I don't feel obliged to have the position for a long time. My job is to professionalise and restructure the organisation. My job might be to find a new permanent CEO.' Christine made small rings in the water with her hand.

'Does the job require you to live in Norway?' she asked with a low voice. She lifted her gaze from the water to the window. She knew that he looked at her. She had started to get cold, and her underlip was starting to tremble. Her knees were pulled up underneath her chin, and her hands were folded around them.

Charlie leaned backwards, with his upper body resting on his forearms. He looked at her, but then looked outside as well.

'Not necessarily, but I wouldn't mind living here.' He looked at her again.

'I just don't want to say no to other opportunities …that might mean *more* to me than the *job*.' He leaned towards her, now just inches away from her. She looked at him, and he leaned closer to her still, with the intention of maybe kissing her blue, shaking lips. She liked to be close to him, and she wanted to be near him. It was such a long time since she had felt the attention Charlie was giving her. It was so long since Henrik had looked at her that way. *Am I really about to do this? Am I about to kiss someone else than Henrik?* She didn't want the moment to end, but she just couldn't kiss someone else than Henrik, as she realised that it was all wrong, what she was about to do. It was wrong of her to be so close to Charlie was well. She slowly pulled back and looked out the window again. Charlie sighed and looked into the pool. His head was hanging, and she knew he was disappointed, but he didn't leave. He must have felt that she really wanted to be close to him. She was glad she hadn't rejected him enough to leave.

'Where is Heidi?'

Charlie didn't reply at once. After a while, he said, 'I assume she went to bed.'

'Did you say, "I have to get up early tomorrow morning?"'

'You do not think very highly of your so-called best friend.'

'I do. She just has very bad judgment when it comes to men. Heidi thinks she likes to just sleep around, but she does get emotionally attached. I don't think less of her because she does. She just always thinks the best of people, and that gets her into trouble.'

'Unlike you,' he said.

'I trust very few people, and it takes a long time before I know I can trust them. I'm just not a fool for flirts, like she is. I have a boyfriend.'

'You flirt, though.' Charlie looked at her with a smirk. '…with married men, even.' Christine was embarrassed and wrinkled her nose. 'You flirt too,' she replied.

'No, I don't. I've never been good at that.'

'You flirt with Heidi, and you flirt with me, now.'

'I like hanging out with you. I like being your friend. You make me smile.'

Christine smiled.

'Actually, I went right after you, Heidi stayed with the rest.'

'She likes you.'

'So? You just said she likes everybody.' Christine didn't reply.

'Miss Loveness,' he said in a calm voice. 'Are you jealous?'

'No,' Christine answered quickly, and got up. He got up after her.

'It's nothing to be embarrassed about.' He was laughing.

'I just think Heidi is a good match for you. She is fun, she's blonde and pretty, quirky and very social. And she obviously finds you *hilarious*.'

'Maybe I'm more into shy and intelligent brunettes.' He was standing opposite her and tried to look her in the eyes.

'Most people find me boring. Even the papers.'

'I don't find you boring, at all.'

'That's because you see me as forbidden.'

'I don't.'

'Do I need to remind you that I am seeing someone? Who happens to be your boss' son. Or the chairman of your board.'

'I know.'

'You might become *really* rich staying in this job. The only thing you can't have at the same time, is me. Certainly I can't be worth all that money to you.'

'I just said, I will let anything keep me from choosing my own life. I can always find another job.'

Christine looked at him, wondering if he really meant what he said.

'Can I kiss you?' He whispered.

'Are you willing to give it all up?'

'Are you? I can't stop thinking about you.' He was so close to her now, she could feel his breath.

'I don't know. I shouldn't.'

'But swimming in the middle of the night, flirting and dancing with married men is ok?' he said flirtatiously. She quickly pulled away, realising kissing him would be crossing a line.

'I think I have to get back to bed." She walked over to her robe and took it down from the peg.

He grabbed her shoulder, and she turned around. 'I didn't mean to upset you. I don't mean that you were doing anything wrong.'

She didn't reply and put her coat on over her robe.

'I had a great day with you today," Charlie said. He stood there, slightly looking down at her in his robe, while she was almost fully dressed with her fur cape on. He touched her hand and stroked it gently. Christine sensed he was still trying to kiss her. He bent his head down a little closer to her. She liked having him close to her. She took a deep breath, and smelled him carefully. She didn't pull back, but turned her cheek towards his mouth and stayed close. She didn't want this moment to end. He moisted his lips, and breathed on her, so she felt the warmth from his breath. Then, he kissed her slowly on her cheek. His lips stayed there for a few seconds. They were warm and soft, and she felt a heated sensations spreading around her body. He pulled back slowly, and looked her in the eyes. Their eyes met, and his wet eyelashes looked so tempting to just keep staring into. Charlie must have read her fascination with his eyes as a sign of agreement, and he started to move forward to kiss her mouth, Christine suddenly realised what she was about to do. Christine pulled back, turned around quickly, and picked up her boots before she was quickly out the door. She rushed up the stairs, and barely got her boots on her wet feet before she was out the main door, into the dark winter night.

*

Christine locked herself in her room as quickly as she could. She tossed off her boots and threw her cape and bathrobe off onto a small chair by the door. On her way to the bathroom, she saw her phone blinking on her nightstand. There were fifteen missed calls from Henrik. She stood there, watching over her phone. Her swimsuit was dripping. It started to ring again. She just watched it. She couldn't answer it, it was like her fingers were frozen. Christine went into the bathroom and laid her phone on the edge of the sink. She took off her swimsuit and looked at herself in the mirror. Her hair was dripping wet, her skin was pale and reddish from the quick run through the cold. She felt ugly. She couldn't put a finger on why, she just felt so ugly. She tilted her head, and then leaned into the mirror. She looked herself in the eye. Her pale blue eyes looked dead, the skin around her eyes looked old. She felt like the most worn out twenty-six-year-old she had ever seen. Christine got into the shower. She didn't know for how long she stood there. She used all the soap, but forgot to wash her hair properly, and just let the water run over it.

*

When she woke up a couple of hours later, Christine called the reception to ask if it was necessary to go to the reception to check out, which is wasn't, and she also asked if they could call her a taxi. She packed her suitcase quickly and went outside. It was a beautiful winter morning. The sun was still below the horizon, but it was getting lighter. Christine didn't know what time it was, but she was assuming it was about seven. She could barely hear the taxi arrive, as the snow covered every noise. She got in and didn't look back.

*

As she entered the door at home in Oslo, Christine picked up her phone and called Henrik. He answered.

'Hi,' she said carefully. 'How are you? Are you ok?'

'I can't sleep,' he answered, and she could hear he was crying.

'But sweetie, it's morning now, so maybe you should get your things, go to the airport, and I can help you sleep here. You know that always helps.' Christine knew this drill from so many times before, but it felt like a battle every single time.

'I'm not sure if I can manage to get there, I just want to sleep. Maybe never wake up.'

'I know, but sleep helps,' she said. She could hear his deep breaths.

'Sweetie, do you have a t-shirt on? Just put on your jeans as well. Do you know where your passport is? Just go and see if it's where you think it is. Let's just take one step at a time. I will be here all the way, and I will be at the airport to pick you up. When you get here, you can sleep for as long as you want, and I will take care of you. I will stroke your head. That always helps.'

The Third Year

The Perfect Facades

Christine stopped in front of the green door. She took a deep breath and enjoyed the silence. Her carry-on was beside her, and the sound that it had made on the cobblestone street was unbearable. She rang the bell. It was completely quiet inside. She rang again. It was still completely quiet inside. Christine knew Henrik wasn't home, but she didn't stop. He hadn't returned her calls all the way from the airport, and she knew she wouldn't find him here either. She knew Henrik was aloof, and she hadn't spoken to him since Tuesday. Admittedly, she hadn't tried very hard to reach him, but she *had* texted him her arrival times yesterday. She knew he wouldn't be representable for dinner tonight, so she hadn't been too eager to remind him of it. She also felt more comfortable showing up to the event single. Again. She started to look for her keys in her bag. It was too big to really find anything without emptying the whole bag on the entrance mat. She knew they weren't there, but she emptied the whole bag just to be sure. She was getting more annoyed. *Why didn't I bring a key?* Christine vaguely remembered that Henrik had hidden a key outside during his university days, but she couldn't remember exactly *where*. She looked under the flowerpot, under the mat, behind the rubbish bin, and in the roof gutter she could just barely reach, in case he had hidden it there. *Where the hell was he?* Christine tried to look through a tiny gap in the curtains. Maybe he was hung over and sleeping on the sofa, but she couldn't see him. Christine's pulse was rising, and she could feel the anger building up inside her.

'Argh!' She let out some steam. It was no problem for her to check into a hotel, she just knew it would be embarrassing to hand the receipt to the accountant, as questions would be raised why she didn't stay in Henrik's flat. She didn't want to lie to Heidi where she was staying either. Christine sat down on the entrance mat, hoping it was dry. She sat there with her knees under her chin. All the surrounding houses were so charming and lovely in their imperfectness. They were all very well taken care of, with flowerpots and benches. It was one of London's most expensive areas, and most people could only dream of living on this street. As she sat there, Christine couldn't help but wonder: *do all these neighbours also have great facades for a life, but a messy interior?* She started to google hotels nearby. Christine knew she could stay with Harald and Wenche, but she didn't feel like telling them she had no idea where Henrik was. Again. *Maybe I should just stay at the hotel Heidi is staying at?* She might as well tell her the truth and be honest with one person at least, knowing she would have to lie to everyone else. Christine tried calling Heidi. There was no answer. She was probably still in the air, as she was on a later flight. Heidi had decided she would stay at another hotel than where the rest of the office was staying, since it was both cheaper and closer to her favourite little shopping street. After some thought, Christine was quite happy she could hide at the hotel with Heidi, and no one else. She dragged her carry-on back to the main road and tried to see if she could find a taxi.

"Is it possible for you to take me to the Number Sixteen Hotel, sir? I believe that's what it's called, it should be right off Old Brompton Road," she said as she stepped in. Christine let her mind drift away as she looked out the window. She had dreaded the dinner tonight for a few months now. Ever since her meltdown last year, she had dreaded seeing Charlie again. She hadn't seen him many times in the office, because she had checked his calendar and managed to have lots of meetings, preferably out of the office, wherever he was in town. On the other hand, she had accepted and been present at all video conference meetings with him. It was a completely different thing, and the screen always showed the whole meeting room. Charlie still looked very handsome on camera as well, but there was no real eye contact, no proper way of having a real conversation, and no proper way of letting him flirt with her.

Christine knew that day last year had been a low point for her, and she knew she was exceptionally vulnerable that day. No wonder she had fallen for his charm. She had been completely overlooked and forgotten by Henrik, and she had let her mind go into this downward spiral of gossip and headlines. Since last year, there hadn't been one single headline about Henrik and Zoey. Her relationship with Henrik hadn't improved at all, but she had no proof of cheating, and they were just living parallel lives.

Henrik's health hadn't been great this year, but he had still managed to be travelling a lot. He had been away at his usual retreat for a couple of weeks and went on a long holiday in the Caribbean after that. Then he went to Los Angeles for at least a month to visit friends and gather people for his next project. And then, he had needed a holiday after that. He went home in between to see her, but in Christine's mind, it had all been a holiday for him that year, and a new low in September. Henrik had been okay the last time she had spoken to him, but now she was afraid he would crash again soon. She knew that if he was having too much fun, and was too inspired, too enthusiastic, and too busy to talk to her, tides were about to turn. He usually went under the radar before he would call her for help again.

Christine had started to feel that this was how the relationship would be for the rest of their lives. While her other friends were growing up, getting married and sharing memories, she was existing and Henrik was living. She had accepted the situation for a long time, but she wasn't happy, or living the life that *she* wanted. She had started to feel that she was on a leash for Harald, and Henrik was free as a bird. She filled her weeks with work, and tried to enjoy her weekends with her friends, but she wondered how it would be to actually live with her boyfriend, and to share a life. She was starting to realise that she and Henrik would ever get to that point.

And now, she was dreading meeting Charlie. Christine was afraid it would be so awkward to see him again with everyone around, and she was wondering if it was best to just face the situation and get it over with. Then she didn't have to feel like everyone was watching her. And she knew she would be placed close to him, as they had been at the same table the last two years. She could always kill time before dinner with some never-ending shopping with Heidi, or she could get the uncomfortable encounter with Charlie over with.

She started to write a text.

Hi. Want to join me for lunch today? Henrik is busy, and …

No. It was a bad idea to lie. She deleted the last sentence. She had to be a bit polite, so she added **how are you? Hope all is well** at the beginning. She quickly pressed send, put the phone in her bag, and closed her eyes. She regretted sending the text already and tried to think about something else.

'Lovely day, eh?' It took her a second to realise it was the taxi driver who spoke to her.

'Yes, it's beautiful to see the sun for a change. I've heard it has been raining for days here.'

'Yeah, it's been 'orrible. If ye weren't depressed before the bloody pleasure and pain, it certainly made ye depressed.' Christine was now worried about Henrik. It was strange; she was more worried about him when she was physically closer to him, and she knew that if he was on his way down, depressing weather wouldn't help.

'So, what're ya doin' in London?'

'Oh, I have this work dinner thing.' Christine knew she couldn't hide her lack of enthusiasm.

'Must be rather uncle josh if ya travelled ter be garn ter it, but ya make it sound like it's a prosecution your attendin'.

Christine didn't really understand what he said, but she continued. 'Well, I'm not looking forward to it, really.'

'Oh, sum people ya don't wanna meet? 'Ave ya been mixin' business wit pleasure?' The taxi driver was looking at her with a grin in the rear-view mirror.

'NO.' Christine did not want to have that talk with the driver. She avoided the mirror, and fixed her gaze out the window.

'Ye know, ya should always put pleasure before business. Ya can always find a job that ya okay wif, a way ter pay your bills - it's 'arder ter find someone you like. Wot is the worst thin' that can 'appen? Ya lose ya job?'

'I beg your pardon?' She said, still looking out the window.

'Ya job. Would it be terrible ter lose it?'

Losing just her job sounded really tempting, but Christine realised she had already mixed business with so-called-pleasure when she accepted to work for Harald. As she stepped out of the taxi, she was glad she was done with the taxi driver, who most certainly hit a nerve. She tried to call Heidi again, but was sent straight to voice mail. As she walked inside, Christine thought about whether to leave her bags and wait for Heidi to share a room with her, or get her own room. She was about to call Heidi again, when a text from Charlie lit up the screen.

Absolutely ready for lunch, where are you?

Christine smiled as she walked into the hotel. She simply asked for a room. No story, no 'maybe my boyfriend will be home later', and she did not ask about Heidi's reservation. She wrote back to Charlie:

How about Colbert at Sloane Square? I can be there in half an hour.

The reply came instantly.

Perfect.

Christine went up to her room, took off her wool coat , and emptied out half her bag. She looked at herself in the mirror, and she felt okay. On her way out, she called to reserve a table, in her own name. She started to walk, and she knew it would take more time than she had to get to the restaurant.

*

As she walked through the door of the restaurant, she could see the back of Charlie's head. He sat there in a striped suit and his hair was combed perfectly to the side. She looked around and saw that everyone in the restaurant was nicely dressed. Christine had her biker boots on and had tried to get her coat to drape over her shoulders like Heidi had shown her. At least her sweater was showing her décolletage pretty nicely. She pulled out her hair-tie and tried to toss her hair about without garnering too much attention. He must have heard her approaching, or maybe he had just been turning his head around every so often, looking out for her.

'Hello, It's good to see you!' He stood up and gave her a kiss on each cheek. His big bright smile made her feel very welcome, and the nerves she had felt earlier about seeing him privately were completely gone.

'Good to see you too!,' she said as she sat down.

'I'm starving. The *chevre salat* is very good here, I really do recommend it, but you have probably been here before, as it was your suggestion, and I would never tell you what to order anyway.' Charlie was obviously nervous, and it made Christine smile.

'I don't think I've ever seen you in your London workwear. You're always a lot more casual in Oslo. Those pinstripes suit you.'

'Thank you,' he smiled. As their eyes met, she noticed that his shoulders dropped. "This straight jacket is a must here in London, sadly. Maybe one day I can work in whatever I want. I guess it will be a sign of my independence. How are you, though? Just landed, or did you come last night, maybe?'

Christine didn't know what to tell him. Should she lie? Or just tell the truth?

'Shall we order first?' she blurted out. She looked down at the menu. *What am I doing? I' almost kissed him, avoided him for a year, and I thought it was a good idea to have lunch? Why would I think it was so awful to say hello to him tonight? This is MUCH worse.*

'You know, every time I land in Oslo, I want to take the route we took together,' Charlie said. 'That was such a beautiful trip. And I can't really remember where we went. That day felt like it wasn't real. I must admit I didn't know how to act after that.'

It was as if he knew she regretted this meeting. After that, the conversation went much more smoothly. Charlie talked about the office a bit, how it was funny how close they both were to Harald during work hours, but how little they spoke to each other. And then, he said:

'I find it a bit weird that, theoretically, I am your boss. Up until now, I have used my time to implement the strategy for all offices overseas, and there hasn't been any reason for looking into your department, but that might change as Harald is withdrawing even more. How do you feel about that?'

Christine had gotten used to the fact that he was her boss, but she had been avoiding him every time he was in Oslo, which he must have noticed. 'I'm completely okay with that of course. Why would't I be?' *Oh, he must know I am lying!*

'Well, just so you know at least, I will be spending more time at your office, and I will require your attendance more often. In Oslo.'

Christine just nodded.

'Good. We have that sorted then. So, I need to pick up my dinner jacket from the dry cleaner before I have a meeting back at the office. Could I tempt you with a coffee to go and a walk? We'll go past the dry cleaners.'

As they were walking out, Christine first and Charlie after, a familiar face looked right at them. Christine was startled, it was Alex Weeum-Hansen. She felt a chill run down her back. Even though it was not improper for her have had a work lunch with Charlie, she just didn't like meeting Alex in general.

'What a lovely surprise to run into you here, Alex!' Christine exclaimed, surprised at her own false enthusiasm.

Alex got up and gave her a kiss on each cheek. 'How random

to run into you two here,' he said smugly, and a tad suspiciously.

'Not really, we might as well have a work lunch, we work together, remember? So, are you ready for tonight?' Christine was quick with her reply and changing the subject.

'Yes, indeed. Really looking forward to a smaller group tonight, *crème de la crème*, right? The inner circle of VIPs.'

'Well, don't flatter yourself too much. The invitations were the same as always, there were just fewer people who would take the weekend trip to London.' Christine was surprised of how condescendingly she spoke to him. She tried smooth over it by saying, 'But of course, being in London, a few other local guests had the opportunity to come this year as well, so the evening won't be lacking.'

'See you tonight, then. Enjoy your lunch.' Charlie cut off the conversation. As Charlie held the door open for Christine, he whispered, 'I can't stand that guy. You don't have to be polite to him. Harald only cares about his parents.'

'I know. He's always been after Henrik, and I feel he can always misinterpret things on purpose and start some rumours.' Charlie gave her an understanding look. As they stood out on the pavement of Sloane Square, Christine felt her phone ring in her pocket. She looked at the screen, without Charlie seeing it. It was

Heidi.

'Don't you want to answer it?'

'I'll take that later."

They started to walk. After the pleasant small-talk, Charlie finally dared to ask about what he seemed the most interested in. 'So … How is Henrik? Do you know how his new project is doing?'

'I really don't know. He doesn't tell me that much. He has his world, and I have mine. They're quite different, and there is no point in discussing work, as neither of us has any clue how to help if there is a problem.'

'Hmm. I guess people are different. I myself would like to discuss my work-life with my life partner. But that is just me.'

Christine did agree with him, she would have loved it if Henrik shared his work problems with her. It was a way of understanding each other better and taking part in one another's lives.

'I just find it difficult to support him when it is such a different business, with such different type of people involved. It's so nice when the relationship also becomes a clear break from work, a different life. I'm not sure which way I would prefer it if it was just up to me.'

'I guess a lot of people have parallel lives, and jobs they don't speak about at home. Are you sure he is not some sort of James Bond kind of guy? It wouldn't surprise me; he most certainly looks like one.

'I guess that would be a better excuse, wouldn't it. On some level I hope he *is* working on something top secret - then all of his travelling would be a bit more justified.'

'We'll, no relationship is perfect. I just hope you find a balance that works for both of you.'

'Relationship expert, are you now? Still single?"

"*Touché*," he said and smiled. There was a long pause. As they walked along the green by the Saatchi Gallery, Charlie started to speak again.

'So … I lied. I don't have a meeting back at the office.' Christine smiled at him.

'Is there an imaginary jacket at the dry cleaners as well?'

'That part is actually true. The reason I am telling you is because I was hoping we could take a walk, maybe a bit of a detour, because the weather is so nice and the company is even better. Do you have any plans before dinner?'

'Well … I guess I should tell you, since you admitted your lie.' She took a deep breath. 'I was supposed to stay at Henrik's, but I don't know where he is.'

Charlie raised his eyebrows, but he didn't say anything. She continued:

'In fact, I haven't spoken to Henrik since Tuesday. Which shouldn't be a norm in any relationship, but it is in mine. I couldn't get hold of him last night, nor this morning. I don't know where he is. We were supposed to be together this weekend, or at least that was what *I* had planned. Since I forgot my key, I left my bags at what I believe is Heidi's hotel. I doubt he will show up at dinner.'

'Is this really normal for you?'

'Yes, sort of, it has *become* the norm. Sometimes we don't speak for a while, but I get an occasional text. When he disappears from the face of the earth, he is usually getting sick again. You know, a massive high before a hell of a low. He doesn't want to be found. This is sadly happening more and more often, and I might as well be honest about it to the ones I know will keep quiet.'

'I am sorry, Christine. It sounds like you have had a terrible year.'

'I guess so. My relationship might seem like a joke, but Henrik's mental health is not a joke at all. I am still hanging in there, for his sake, but I can't keep pretending it is a good relationship. For better or for worse, right?'

'That's when you are married, and still it is up to you, really. I just hope that he treats you nicely when he is well at least, that the better part of your relationship makes it worth it."

Christine knew the answer but wasn't ready to say it out loud. She looked out at the park. Charlie must have felt Christine was done talking about it, and politely changed the subject.

'Do you mind if we quickly stop by my place so I can get out of this straight-jacket? It's not too far.'

Perfect or Psycho?

'So, here it is, the bachelor pad. Prepare yourself for dark walls and freaky art. Oh, and there are mirrors everywhere, and black silk sheets.' Charlie stopped in front of a small door in a red brick street. His place was one of the smaller ones on the street, not that it wasn't impressive. It had huge panes of glass instead of bay windows, and it looked like it could have been an artist's studio centuries ago. It was less impressive than Harald's townhouse, but bigger than Henrik's. Christine didn't dare to say that Charlies description of a bachelor pad, sounded like her home. This place was the opposite. It looked like a fashionable family home from a magazine. The red brick house had black and white tiles in front, two big pots of what seemed to be olive trees, and a row of something that could blossom into lavender in front of the windows. The wrought iron was newly painted, and even the rubbish bin looked perfect in shiny black. The pizza box behind it was the only sign of a young man living there.

'What on earth is that doing here? It's not mine. My neighbour pretends it's mine.' Charlie was jokingly referring to the pizza box as he unlocked the door. The house looked narrow from the outside, but as they stepped in, the dimensions of the place was grand. It was a classic townhouse, light and airy, and you could almost smell the newly painted surfaces. Christine took a look around in the hallway. The house had kept all the classical details, but the lighting and furniture was contemporary, while still being elegant and sedate.

'This is a massive place!" exclaimed Christine. "Do you have a secret family that you haven't told me about? Why do you have all this space?'

'Do I come across as a bit creepy? Do I seem like the guy who's desperate for a family? The truth is, I bought this place a couple of years ago, and it was pretty run down. Ben lives just around the corner. We used to hang at the pub on the corner when we were younger. I bought this and thought I might rent some floors out. Then, my sister needed a place to stay as she had an internship, she stayed longer than expected, and it was nice to have a place where friends and family could stay over. I stay at the top, and the kitchen is all the way down, so the rest of the bedrooms I just keep closed. So there's no need to spend money on a gym membership. I use all my energy running up and down."

Christine looked at him with a tilted head, and raised her eyebrows, like she didn't quite believe his explanation.

'Nice shawl' she said sarcastically, as she noticed a pale blue silk shawl hanging on a chair. As she said it, she instantly understood that it was not his sisters. Charlie blushed and started mumbling:

'Ah, yes, just follow the stairs down to the kitchen, help yourself to whatever you want, and I'll go upstairs and change.'

Christine went down the stairs. They were covered in light beige carpets, and the newly sanded oak underneath was visible at the sides. The balustrade was of polished brass, and the railing was of oiled oak. The kitchen looked like it had just been featured in some minimalist magazine. It was at the same level as the garden, and there were huge stained-glass doors separating them.

The room was filled with light. Christine looked around. It was all so perfect. She opened a cupboard to check if it was just a fake, that there was nothing inside. Everything was there. Cups, pots and pans, knives of every shape. Everything was in perfect order. It wasn't necessarily the neatness that freaked her out, he probably had a maid cleaning twice a day, but it scared her maybe more that it was a perfect family home, without a family.

'Would you care for a glass of water or a cup of tea?'

Christine was startled, as she heard Charlie's voice right behind her. She looked around, but he wasn't there.

'Press the speaker button on the display next to the fridge,' he continued.

'Okay.' She went over to the display and pressed the button. 'Hello?'

'Hi, I just had it fixed. It has never worked, so I just wanted to test it. No so easy to do when you are by yourself. I didn't mean to scare you.'

'You didn't scare me too much, but your kitchen does. I can't decide if it is perfect or psycho.'

'I have never heard that one before.'

'Well, I am wondering if you are the "perfect man without

your perfect housewife", or if you are "perfect with a psycho secret."

'Check out my fridge, then.'

'Is that where you keep your murdered neat-freak of a wife?'

'You'll see.'

She opened the door. It was filled with bottled water and nothing else.

'If you're trying to argue that you are not psycho, I am sad to inform you that this really doesn't help.'

'Open the freezer then.'

She opened the door, and all she could see was dozens of boxes of pre-made dinners, mostly pasta.

'So you're definitely not perfect man without the perfect housewife.'

She could hear him run down the stairs, and all of a sudden, he was in the kitchen with her.

'I've barely put a kettle on in this kitchen.' He had changed into jeans and a shirt and he put his sweater over his head as he spoke.

'You shouldn't think of me as "psycho", but this house does

attract some "not-so-sane-housewife-prospects" like my decorator. She asked me if I wanted to rent the place out fully-furnished. I thought of that as sofa and a dining table.'

'So what happened?'

'Fully-furnished apparently means all of the things you will never use, because you forget them the one time you have to use them. For example, I have sixteen of these things you put a slice of lemon into, so your guest don't have to use their fingers when squeezing a lemon over their food.'

'Did you decorator take a percentage of each item she put into this house? Or did she secretly try to become your wife?'

'Ha! Maybe both? But that strategy of pretending to be posh to be suitable was a strategy that backfired. She took the hint when I questioned why on earth I needed nine different kinds of glasses for sixteen guests, when I would only serve beer from bottles. That's when I let her go. It was also when I got the invoice.'

'Such a shame. She sounded great.'

'Yes, so down-to-earth. Not high maintenance at all.'

'So, if you have a girl home with you, she has to drink wine from the bottle?'

'I do have glasses for wine. It's hilarious though. The wine cabinet is super expensive, and holds the perfect temperature and all that, but I have only ever had cheap plonk in there; you know, the type of wine that you only take because there is some three for two deal of some kind. I fill the glasses up at the counter, and when I come over, they always brag about the wine. They just expect it to be super expensive.'

'*They*? How many women *are* you dating?'

'I'm not commenting on that. The wine is the test, though. There will never be expensive wine in that cabinet, but my cheese grater is as expensive as a first class transatlantic ticket.'

'That's a great pickup line. Want to come to my place and see my cheese grater? It's the Rolls Royce of graters.'

He smiled at her. 'I would never use cheesy pick-up lines.'

'Is that so? So, what do you call this line then: "Oh, I am terribly sorry to ask, but how's you bum doing?" Christine imitated Charlie's accent, and overdid it in a clumsy Hugh Grant way.

'I really did say that. That's so embarrassing. It a good thing you had a boyfriend, otherwise I have to blame my failure on my very bad choice of words.'

Christine was laughing, and hoped he wouldn't point out that she remembered something he had said to her two years ago.

'In my defence,' Charlie continued, 'it is a lot harder than you think. Girls like you can probably go up to any guy, attractive or not, and say one completely random word, and they would still want to shag you.'

'That's not true!'

'After the dinner tonight we can meet my friends afterwards at our usual pub, and we will test my theory.'

'I won't feel sorry for you, Charlie. After you become a regular in stylish magazines, like Tatler.. I'm sure you have to bring one of those electric mosquito rackets with you to keep the girls away from you."

'That is actually not such a bad idea… The thing is, they ones that attack come towards me at an intense speed, and you know, they're so fake they have turned orange.'

Christine laughed. She knew he was talking about girls who he had no interest in at all, celebrity girls from reality-tv. Heavy drinkers with huge boobs and sky-high heels were probably not his cup of tea.

'I'll protect you tonight then, from the attack of the monstrous Oompa-Loompas.'

'There is another kind as well, the young Sloane rangers that are straight out of uni, and are panicking because they did Art History, and are realising their fathers are not as well off as hoped, and they need to marry way before they turn thirty years of age, to keep up appearances and their lifestyle. Because to work for a living was not their plan, God forbid. *Tatler* is their marriage bible.'

'I assume your decorator was in that category?'

'Yes, indeed. It would be great, you know, if I give you a hint and you pretend to be my girlfriend.'

'Are these girls a common problem for you when you're out?'

'Lately, it's sort of exploded. Now I get approached by girls who are either are not allowed to drink, or ladies who should not be *allowed* to drink.'

'What article was that after? Do you have it? Can I read it?' Christine found this extremely funny and started to look around for a magazine in the pile of paper at the end of the counter.

'Why are you so interested in this? Isn't Henrik featured in these things all the time?'

'I guess so. But with him it seems so *ironic*. It feels like it is a mockery, most eligible bachelor… First of all, since he is not married, he is by their definition single. He is neither desirable nor suitable for marriage. I am very glad on your behalf that your stock is up. I look forward to seeing it in action tonight.'

'Oh, don't expect too much. Those lists are pretty ironic for me too.'

'Why is that? Because you think girls can't find you attractive unless they have read the article?'

'It certainly doesn't help that whenever I am at a pub the guys are with me. The guys have been giving me such a hard time about it, and it just makes it really uncomfortable to approach girls I like. So the articles have not been very helpful at all.'

'Well, I hope you weren't planning on casually dropping into conversation that you're on this hottie list to a potentially great girl who hasn't read about you? No one likes a person who is smug.'

'I guess not. I managed to sneak it into conversation with you, though.'

'Yes, you did. I hope you're not trying to impress me or anyone else with it.'

'Well, you're with Henrik. He's on these lists all the time. Why are you still with him, then?' Charlie was serious.

Christine took a deep breath and looked a Charlie. She tried to meet his eyes. She sighed and replied

'I got together with Henrik before he was known. These lists put Henrik on this pedestal, the fact that he is known, and is described as perfect in the media, is a big negative factor for me. His wealth has nothing to do with why I am still with him. I really hope that the girl you decide to be with one day will be with you *despite* those lists, not *because* of it. So, are you ready for a walk?'

*

The air was crisp, and the sky was still beautiful and rather mild. As they walked outside, Charlie seized the opportunity to talk about Henrik.

'So, why are you still with Henrik then?'

Christine smiled and looked at him. She knew that this was a mystery to Charlie.

'I stay with him because he is my family, and he needs his family. I am there for him. He needs me to help him handle his life, and I need him.'

'I know you pretty well now, I think, and to me, it doesn't really look like you need him as much.'

'That's because I am comfortable with you, I am scared to

death in social settings. I am usually a mess, but he teaches me how to relax, how to enjoy life. I have to admit, it is a while ago now.'

'I hope he does as much for you, as you do for him. I mean, it seems so obvious you accepted a job at Harald's because you feel like you owed him, and that it was the right thing to do. Your last job seemed a lot more interesting, and they must have paid you more than what we do. But you didn't dare to negotiate the salary, did you? Because he basically owns your home and pays for your life?'

Christine knew she couldn't lie to Charlie.

'It was an interesting opportunity, and yes, they paid me more at my last job. But I'm interested in his business, and I thought it would be better if I joined the firm rather than Henrik. So, I accepted. The pressure would then be off Henrik. That is important to me, and when you love someone, you don't do things that are selfish all the time. To do something for someone else might seem weak from the outside, but it actually takes a lot of strength.'

Charlie looked at the ground as they walked along the pavement. He started to kick a little rock he saw in front of him. 'Are you happy then? With your choice, I mean. Because, and I say this to you as your friend, it doesn't seem like it. Henrik is travelling all over the world, fulfilling his dream, and leaving you behind. That can't be your dream.'

Christine stopped. "That's harsh," she said in a low voice. Her eyes were filled with tears.

He came closer to her, and looked into her eyes. Her tears stayed in her eyes.

"I'm sorry I stepped out of line, I just think you deserve better, since you put everyone before yourself. Look, I don't think you should accept his behaviour just because he owns your home, or he supported you years ago. Harald and Wenche adore you, they love you like you were their own daughter. But, I am pretty sure they don't want you to stay with their son because of guilt or because you feel like it's the right thing to do."

She didn't reply.

*

The street was still wet although the sun was peeking through the vanilla sky. The warm rays usually made Christine relax. It was just so nice to be in a city that felt a lot more peaceful than at home. The red brick facades felt like they were giving off heat, as if they were a heated chimney. She felt at home, because she knew nobody would recognise her here.

'Where are we going?' she suddenly asked Charlie.

He just smiled at her. 'Trust me, you'll love it.'

*

In the small park, Christine could spot a family playing with a small, brown dog. They were running around so happily. Christine was completely in her own head. Suddenly, a scooter passed them at a great speed, with a mother riding it, and her daughter behind her. Christine was caught completely off guard, and almost lost her balance as Charlie pulled Christine towards him to avoid being hit. They were suddenly very close, Christine was under his arm, and she could feel his short stumble against her head. He felt strong, and although he wasn't that much higher than Christine, she felt very safe in his arms. Startled by her own comfort in his arms, she quickly pulled back. Their eyes met as they were a few inches apart from each other.

'Ah, here we are,' Charlie lifted his head, as if he were pointing somewhere. Christine turned around. They walked into this small café, with a turquoise-painted store front. The windows were covered in frost, and it looked warm and cozy inside.

*

The tiny bell rang. The interior was white chalked walls, with wooden chairs and turquoise tables. The large rough oak counter was filled with baked goods and delicious cakes.

'This is my favourite place,' Charlie said as he walked inside. Christine smiled at Charlie.

'This feels like it should have been on a Caribbean island,' she said enthusiastically.

'But you can bring your dog and you avoid getting sunburnt,' Charlie referred to a girl who sat in the window with her laptop and her dog in her lap.

'Hi Charlie!' Christine could hear a voice behind her. It was the lady behind the counter, her smile was a ray of sunshine.

'Hi Amy! How are you today?' Charlie replied.

'All good, or I *was* at least. Here I've been serving you coffee and scones and hoping that you would take me out on a date, but now that you bring a lady friend to my coffee and scones. I bet she hasn't cooked you so much as a piece of toast.' She was saying it with a cheerful tone.

Charlie was laughing nervously. 'No, ha, I am not dating her. I am her boss, actually. Or she might be *mine* one day. I would love to take you out, Amy, but you know, if it doesn't go well, I'd have to change where I get my Sunday brunch. There are not many places around here that do a good omelette.'

Amy turned to Christine and said, 'If I were you, I would quit my job so you could date him instead.'

Christine just smiled, but out of the corner of her eye, she could see that Charlie was still pretty uncomfortable. As Christine opened the door to go outside again, she took a bite of her scone.

'You see, I love a proper English scone. With clotted cream and strawberry jam. In Norway you always get them too dry, with nuts, seeds and dried fruit. You can't get them like this in Oslo. It must be something to do with the flour.'

'I've got the same problem with cinnamon buns here in London. Some are pretty close, but just not the same. Should I just give up?'

'Maybe. It might be the place that is the X-factor. You know, the one thing missing that you can't describe. It's like when you bring wine or something home from a holiday, and it's just not the same when you have it at home? It is, but the atmosphere is not the same. Some things just can't be replaced.'

'I guess you're right. So should I just accept it, or try to find a second-best?'

'Don't know, it depends on the quality of second-best. I only have scones in England. There's no point having them anywhere else.'

'Good thing you can come to London once in a while then.'

'And you just have to keep coming to Oslo more often.' She smiled at him.

The Advantage of London's Black Cabs

Christine was ready for dinner. She looked in the mirror. All she could see was her dress, her massive tulle dress covered with lots of embroidered flowers. She knew it was extremely expensive, but she hadn't had the strength to argue against Wenche on this one. She was tired of trying to be rational and economical, and somehow she had ended up with the most extravagant dress. She felt like it was a dress only royals would wear. She heard a knock on the door.

'Are you ready?' It was Heidi on the other side of the door.

'Yes,' Christine answered as she opened the door.

'So … have you heard from Henrik yet?'

'No, but now I don't want him to come. I know he is not in a state where he should be there. If he comes, of course he will be the most charming and star of the room, but he is not well. I just hope I hear from him soon. I am ready to go without him.'

'So you just walked around in the streets all day?'

'No, I actually had lunch with Charlie. We had some work to discuss.' Christine knew she was partly lying, but she had remembered they had run into Alex.

'That's nice. I thought you couldn't stand him. You've never been around when he's been in the office, and I didn't see you speak to him last year.'

'I don't have any particular thoughts of him, or if I do, I do find him a bit too perfect. But he is my boss, and I have to speak to him at times.' Christine hoped her lying wasn't too obvious.

'I think he's great, and not because he is successful, but because I find him genuine.' Christine didn't say anything.

'You look amazing by the way. Is that a super expensive dress?'
'Yes, it is. It's itchy, but since there is so much going on, I think it will hide if I spill anything. My mother taught me that patterns are good because they hide stains.'

'Like you will ever wear that again, Christine. God, I want your life sometimes.'

'Well, you know I would rather have worn your dress tonight.'

Heidi was wearing a black, classic dress.

'It's off-the-rack, most likely polyester and two years old, so you can't.'

'Can't have everything I guess,' Christine smiled at Heidi, and they left her room.

*

Christine was enjoying herself at the dinner. She felt comfortable with all the guests, and she enjoyed having Heidi there so she always had someone to go to in case she didn't have anyone to talk to, but that didn't happen. Although she felt like her dress was the centre of attention in the room, she still felt comfortable. She knew they were about to take their seats, but she still hadn't seen Charlie. She stayed in the foyer for a long time, but there was no sight of him. Just as she was about to go in, she felt a tap on her shoulder. She was startled at once, but she knew it was Charlie.

'Hi, I just wanted to say you look great tonight.' As quickly as he said it, he casually continued walking into the dining room. As she sat down, she saw that Charlie was at a table at the opposite end of the room. He smiled at her. She smiled back. The dinner commenced, and every now and then, Christine looked over to Charlie. Every time, he smiled back at her, but he never approached her. The night passed quickly. She felt as if she was glowing, like she had transformed into Henrik that night. She saw

Alex, but tried to ignore him. She didn't need any comments from him. Christine enjoyed the meal, and she had one of Harald's very good friends in London by her side, a man named Angus. Christine had met him on many occasions, and he was fun, charming, and a bit flirty, although married for more than fifty years. He had known Harald almost all his life. She didn't exactly know, but he seemed to own about half of Scotland, or something like that. All of a sudden, Charlie came over to their table to say hello to Angus. He leaned down to speak to him, but he smiled wholeheartedly at Christine while talking.

'So, Charlie! I hear you have been mentioned on all kinds of bacherlor lists lately, and still you have no date with you? How hopeless are you?' Angus was laughing as he said it. Charlie wrinkled his nose.

'Well, I've been busy working for your best friend. You do know that dragging different girls home all the time is quite exhausting after a while!'

'It's all so much fun, everything about sharing a life with someone. All grand events should be enjoyed, from proposing to having children,' said Angus. 'When you do find someone you want to propose to, you should do something spectacular. Like, out of this *world*. You know, like Henrik did. Has Harald told you how he managed to fly a Mexican mariachi band to their island in the Caribbean when he proposed to the lovely Christine here a few weeks ago? Henrik was ecstatic, and told Harald that his whole body was trembling of joy for days afterward. Apparently it was such a massive high."

Christine knew by Charlie's sudden quietness and how his gaze went straight to the floor that he probably didn't know that she was engaged. *Harald didn't tell him? He told Angus and not Charlie?* As Angus went on and on about her and Henrik's engagement, Charlie said nothing. After a few moments, a waiter came up to them, and told Charlie to find his seat, as they had served the main course at his table already. Charlie was probably relieved to leave the table without much further explanation. Charlie avoided Christine for the rest of the dinner. Christine tried to meet his eyes, to explain everything. Didn't he understand that the whole proposal show was part of Henrik's manic behaviour? Did he not listen to Angus' description? The proposal was all about Henrik, and that he wanted to do something fun. She didn't even have a ring. He had forgotten about that, but he had ordered the band to be flown in.

*

She eventually gave up trying to make contact with Charlie, as she assumed he had no interest in speaking to her. After she felt she had mingled enough with guests, Christine found time to chat with Heidi at the bar.

'Not a word from Henrik?'

'No.'

'Aren't you worried? You seem to be quite relaxed about this.'

'To be fair, I am pretty used to this. It's not the first time.' Christine looked around the room and gave her almost empty glass a twirl so the ice cubes made a clear sound. 'And it will most certainly not be the last time.' She took a sip and let the cubes do a small dance around her glass again. Christine was shocked how honest she was with Heidi, as she had usually tried to cover up Henrik's behaviour.

'Well, it's a good thing it's not ruining your night then. I don't think I have ever seen you so comfortable at a party before.'

'Well, I might have learned something from Henrik.' Just as Christine mentioned his name, her phone rang. It was Henrik. She quickly tried to get away from the bar, and went into the corridor and into the ladies room.

'Hello?' She wondered if Henrik was actually calling her or dealing from his pocket.

'Christine? You there?'

'Hi sweetie, how are you?' Although her question should have been *where* he was instead she had learned that she had to go easy on him. Especially since the state he had been in the last time they spoke was definitely a warning sign.

'Should I have been somewhere tonight? Was the dinner tonight?'

'Ehhhm … yes ,and yes.' Christine could hear he was at a party somewhere, since the music in the background was not coming from the bar.

"Oh crap. I'm in Copenhagen."

'What on earth are you doing there? Was that the plan?' Christine was relieved he at least wasn't on his way to her, in a state even Henrik couldn't manage to conceal.

'Oh, you know, my friend convinced me to go to this thing …' She could hear a girl's voice speaking to him, but as it was Danish, she didn't understand much more than that the girl mentioned Henrik's name.

'Shh …' Christine heard Henrik whisper to the girl, as if Christine couldn't hear him. Christine knew Henrik was terribly drunk, as his subtleness and intelligence was at an all-time low. Christine didn't know what to say or do. She felt this confirmed what she had tried to convince herself wasn't true for such a long time. But now that his own drunkenness exposed him, she knew that even she couldn't turn her back on it any longer. He was not interested in her any longer. Although they were recently engaged, she knew it didn't matter. He was with other girls all the time. She knew he had to be sleeping with them as well. In the Caribbean, the sex had been all about him. As if she wasn't there almost, as if he didn't know which girl he was with. There was no connection, and he had done things he should have known she didn't like. It felt like it was a standard procedure, an autopilot of sequences. What she imagined would be the routine of a single man getting laid every weekend, someone just thinking about his own pleasure. As he now didn't even care enough to go away from a girl to speak to her, she felt chill down her spine.

'Just call me sometime tomorrow. Love you,' She managed to say, as she quickly hung up. Christine stood there, watching her phone. Her hand was trembling. All of a sudden, a lady entered the room. Christine pulled herself together, nodded politely to the woman, and walked out. She found her place at the bar next to Heidi quite quickly.

'You all right?' Heidi asked her.

'Now, he doesn't even bother to walk away from those girls when he speaks to me.' Heidi didn't say anything. They just stood there, looking at each other. Eventually Heidi said: 'I think there's a sip or two left here.' She handed Christine a drink.

'Thanks,' Christine said as she drowned the rest of the drink.

'..And I will order you another one.' Heidi turned around to get a hold of the bartender. As Christine stood there, leaning against the bar, drowning her last sip of whiskey sour, Charlie finally looked at her. Just as she had given up speaking to him, he caught her tipping her glass almost upside down, like some pathetic loser trying to get the maximum alcohol out of her drink. She had been so together all night. Christine slowly lowered her glass. She put it down behind her and started walking towards him.

'Hi,' she said in a lowered voice, not knowing how to act.

'Hi,' he answered, without reassuring her with a smile or friendly eyes.

'Enjoying your night?'

'Not terribly. Do you want to get out of here?'

'Yes, please,' she said relieved.

'I'll meet you up front in five minutes?'

'OK, I'll just let Heidi know we're off, so she won't worry.' Christine returned to Heidi, who was speaking to a sweet guy from the Oslo office. She grabbed the drink Heidi had ordered for her and downed it. She tapped Heidi's shoulder.

'Call Charlie to find out which bar we're at. I can't stand being here a minute longer.' Christine tried to leave as smoothly as she could, being as tall as she was and also in heels and a massive ballgown. She got her coat from the cloakroom, and quickly went out the door. Charlie was already in a taxi, and opened the door from the inside. Christine was quite pleased that London had these black cabs. They were ideal for escaping quickly from a scene in a ballgown of tulle.

She sighed and smiled at him. 'Where are we going?'
'I know this great little pub.' He turned to the driver and said, 'Sand's End, please.'

The Perks of Newfound Fame

'So ... you're engaged?' Charlie looked at her with a strained look.

Christine lifted her hand.

'Do you see any ring? Or my fiancée, for that matter? I am as much engaged now as I have been for years. Or maybe I should say I am as *far* from engaged as I have ever been.' Christine looked out the window as they passed St. James's Palace and headed down to the Mall.

'Don't you understand that Henrik's having a manic period?' she continued. 'A band from Mexico, but no ring? Give him a week or two, and he won't even remember it. Or he'll be regretting the whole proposal terribly. I am surprised Harald told Angus.'

Charlie turned around and looked at Buckingham Palace, and after a while he said, 'So how often is he sick now?'

Christine sighed, and said, 'It feels continuously.'

'And how are you doing then?'

Christine looked down at her hands. They were no longer quivering. 'I feel nothing. I feel numb.'

She sat there in her massive gown with embroidery that must have taken months to stitch. In her beautiful and decadent gown, diamonds in her ears and on her wrist, she felt as out of control and unrecognisable as she ever had.

'So what are you going to do about it?' Charlie asked.

'Find a way to take control of my life.'

*

They stopped in front of a small, white house with some garden furniture outside. A few people were shivering outside to enjoy a cigarette. Warm light and what looked like a cosy atmosphere came through the windows of the pub. Charlie opened the oak door for her, and she stepped inside in her massive gown with her coat still on. She regretted going in first the second she stepped in, because everyone looked at her. She turned to Charlie in despair.

'Shall we take those seats by the bar?' He nodded towards the bar, at the middle of the room, like it was completely normal to be in a gown and he in a dinner jacket at the pub. The white room was filled with wooden furniture, and behind the counter were waiters in tartan shirts and the bartender also had a leather apron.

'Cool place. Down-to-earth, but quite fancy at the same time,' she said as she sat down at a stool by the bar.

'Oh, and there's a dog here!' Christine spotted the dog next to a table and noticed that the owner was at a table with very pretty girls. Charlie turned his head in the direction she was looking but didn't comment.

'They've got great drinks here, and scotch eggs if you're hungry. I guess I am allowed to loosen this thing now.' Charlie was starting to untie his bow.

'Absolutely,' Christine said. She saw his chest hair appear as he loosened a few buttons. He was even more gorgeous now, hair still in place, but with the shirt slightly open, and a bowtie hanging loose. She didn't understand why she hadn't realised exactly how extremely handsome he was before. Maybe it was his impeccable image that was loosening up, exposing something more masculine and wild. She had to look at the drinks menu to think about something else. Charlie obviously knew the bartender, and he started to speak to Christine.

'I've never seen Charlie with a girl here, but when he finally brings one, he sure makes the whole place look like a fashion shoot!'

'I do realise the dress is maybe not the regular dress code here,' Christine smiled shyly.

'What I am most curious about though, is why did such a stunner like you want to come here with Charlie?'

Christine wanted to disappear.

'Oh, I'm afraid my outfit makes me look like more of a catch than I really am …'

Charlie tried to be nonchalant and cool: 'She's my colleague actually. And we went to a work thing tonight. Just a night cap on our way home really.'

'Ah, I see.' The bartender raised his eyebrows and then smiled at Christine.

'I would much rather be here, actually. This is such a great place! And if I could get out of this itching dress, that would be great too.'

'Well, I have an extra clean shirt in the back,' the bartender said jokingly.

'That would be great! Can I just go in there?' Christine quickly responded.

'Sure ... its right behind the door ...' The bartender was baffled.

'Charlie, can you give me a hand opening the back?' Christine turned her back towards Charlie, and pulled her head down. Charlie just looked at her neck. Her long neck, with the short hairs that weren't long enough to go into her chignon.

'Go on, Charlie, the zipper is just right there at the top.' Charlie lifted his hand, and it was trembling. He quickly looked at the bartender, to see if he was watching, but the bartender was pretending to look for a towel or something.

'I just need you to pull it down an inch or two, so I can pull it down myself in the ladies room.' Christine was in a hurry. The numbness had turned into an itch, and she couldn't get out of her dress fast enough. Charlie pulled the zipper down, and quickly replied: "There you go." He quickly started looking at the drinks menu as if nothing had happened. Christine rushed off, grabbed the shirt behind the door to the kitchen, and went to the ladies room. It wasn't easy to fit her massive dress into a booth, so she pulled down the back zipper in front of the wash basins. She let the top of the dress down, just hanging around her waist. The silk slip she still had on underneath was see through, so she quickly put the shirt on, so that no one would come in and see her in her bra. The shirt was without a doubt too big, but she buttoned a few buttons, rolled up the sleeves, and tied the bottom of the shirt around her waist. She looked at herself in the mirror. In a hurry, she pulled a paper towel out of the dispenser and started to wash off her face. She stayed away from the mascara, so as to not look like a mess, but she was amazed at how much foundation and eyeshadow she had put on. The huge tulle skirt of the gown was of course still out of place at a pub, but she felt relaxed in this, and it looked at least more Christmas Cosy than New Year's Glamourous. As long as they were sitting down, she didn't mind the high heels either.

*

When she came back to the main room, there was a woman, mutton-dressed-as-lamb, with her hands all over Charlie. She was at least ten years older than him, and by the looks of it, she had maybe had a couple drinks too many, a few too many times.

Christine stopped close by, without Charlie or the woman knowing, but Eddie, the bartender, saw that she stood right behind them. She smiled at Ed, and Ed smiled back at her.

'I know you are a very popular man these days …' the woman said in a very flirtatious voice.

'Ahh,' Charlie seemed embarrassed. He hesitated and looked down at the counter. 'I only try to do my work.'

'I know, I am all about my work myself. You know, working all the time is not good. I bet you get really tense, don't you?'

'Oh, yeah, a run or a drink is a great stress relief at the end of the day.'

She was laughing, clearly not thinking about that: 'It's not good for you to drink, but there are other ways to get some tension relief that *are* good for you. You know, like massages. I am pretty good at giving them.'

'Ahem …' Charlie face was red, and he was looking at Ed for help. Ed was pretending to be busy, chopping lemons, but Christine could sense from his smile that he too was following the conversation.

'And I know a few other ways to get some tension out, you know, the best stress relief …' At this point her hand was on his neck. Christine smiled at Ed who had noticed her presence. She then popped her head in between Charlie and the lady.

'Hi, I don't believe we've met?' Christine put her hand in front of her to greet the woman, who was clearly baffled.

'I'm Sarah … I was actually just on my way to the loos.' The woman couldn't get away from them fast enough. Christine sat down at her stool again.

'Enjoying the perks of your newfound fame, I assume?' she asked mockingly.

'Thank you,' Charlie said, clearly relieved. 'How long were you standing there?'

'Long enough to be entertained, quite funny to see you that uncomfortable. This is the type you were trying to tell me about. You know, you are basically just experiencing what most decent-looking girls experience with older men.'
Charlie smiled: 'So, you are compare me to a pretty twenty-year-old girl?'
'Yes, that's why they are so rude. It's not because they are full of themselves, it's because it's the only way to keep creepy guys away. You have to do the same: be rude, arrogant and ignore them.'

'Is that the only way?'

'Yes, unless you want to leave every time.'

'Must be tough to be a girl."

Don't worry, you'll get used to being rude. It will grow on you. Or just have a friend that is prettier than you, I had Heidi. Or just say you have a girlfriend.'

Charlie looked at her, and opened his mouth, but stopped before he said anything. He just gave her a comforting look. She wrinkled her nose.

A message beeped and lit up Christine's phone, interrupting the awkward moment.

Christine looked at her phone. "So … Heidi's not coming, apparently she's having a drink with someone..'

'So it's just me and you, then. The guys are not coming either, they're at some dinner party, and they haven't even had dessert yet.'

'So that means all responsibility is on you, Charlie.'

'What responsibility?'

'The responsibility to help a friend drown her sorrows and make her forget that she has a shitty boyfriend. Make her forget how pathetic she has been for not realising that the relationship has been over for years, when the rest of the world have clearly known for quite some time.'

'I think I can handle that task.' He signalled to Ed for two more gin and tonics. 'We need drinks, and then we'll play the game we always play when one of the guys is dumped.'

'What sort of game?'

'We start with "most attractive movie star", then "most attractive Bond girl" – but we'll do "favourite Bond actor" in your case, most attractive tv personality, and finally, most attractive person you know but haven't dated. You have to drink for each name you mention.'

'I think I can handle that game.' She lifted her glass.

*

After a while, Ed turned off the lights.

'Sorry guys. You're the last people here, and it's been a while since I said it was the last round.' Christine started to unbutton her shirt, which silenced Charlie completely. He just stood there, getting a glimpse of her breasts in her black lace bra.

Ed stopped her saying: 'Oh, don't worry, you can stop by another day with it.'

'Oh, thanks!' Christine turned to Charlie, who was still in a shock. 'I'm sorry, you were saying what?' She realised he was still flabbergasted by her sudden mini striptease.

'Don't worry, Im not *that* drunk. I'm just Scandinavian. Please, don't act like you haven't seen a girl's bra before. Besides, I am *engaged*.' She regretted it as she said it. His face turned serious, and he turned around to paid the bill. He got up, and took his coat on. Then he finally said:

'We should get you a taxi.'

*

'We didn't finish that game. You know, that celebrity game.' Christine tried to make him smile, but he kept his serious face.

'Well, it wasn't as fun as it is with the guys. There is actually a limit to how many Sean Connery pros and cons I can take.'

'I'm sorry. It did put me in a better mood.'

'I'm glad I could be of assistance.' He said politely, avoiding her eyes. He was focused on finding a taxi down the street.

'I didn't finish, though.'

'I am actually not ready to hear twenty minutes of handsome Hollywood star discussions with you until we find you a taxi.'

'Wow, what happened? Did I say something to upset you?'

He sighed and stopped looking for taxis.

'I have to be honest with you. I thought I could handle it, being your friend, but I can't. I've seen you in a bad relationship with Henrik for years, and I think every time that it will change, that you will leave him. Then I learn tonight that you are engaged, which felt like a dagger through my heart, because it is further from breaking up than you have ever been. Then you say it isn't for real, but then you say it again. I can't do this anymore, waiting around like some idiot. So I can't be your best friend, discuss handsome movie stars and have you change in front of me.'

'Oh…' she turned quiet.

Then she started speaking in a low voice: 'I just wanted to say that the last challenge, the person I find attractive that I haven't dated, well, I think my answer is … *you.*' Christine said quietly.

'Oh… okay… thanks.' Charlie blushed. It was then quiet for a while, neither of them knowing what to say or do.

'So, shall we find a taxi for you?'

'Yes, maybe you can just walk me up to the road, and I'll see if I can find one there? It's freezing, and I would rather be moving.'

'Sure,' he said. They walked along the street, Christine with her hands in her pockets. She could feel Charlie trying to walk closer to her. Then he walked a few yards behind her. Then he was next to her again.

'Can I ask you something?' he finally said.

'Sure.'

'Can you stop?' She stopped and looked at him.

'Can I have a kiss?' There was a long pause.

'You're asking for a kiss?' asked Christine.

'Yes.'

'Didn't you just say that it felt like a dagger through your heart when you learned that I was engaged today?'
'Yes, but I just would really like a kiss from you, because I like you. Maybe it will help me get over you.'

'You think a kiss from me will make you get over me?"

'Probably not. I just really like you. I want to see what the fuzz inside me is all about. It might just go out of me.'
She leaned in and closed her eyes. She stopped close to his nose. She liked the smell of him. How could she not have smelled him properly before? She was wondering if she should pull away. She shortly opened her eyes, to see if his were open. As they were closed, she felt she couldn't disappoint him now. She gave him a small kiss on the lips. They were soft and cold, and he tasted like something great she had never tasted before. Surprised by how

much she actually liked to kiss him, she pulled back quicker than she had intended, and opened her eyes. His were open as well.

'Thank you… Let's find you a taxi, then.'

She was certain he was just being polite, because the way he had smelled her too had to be real. As he was about to walk away from her, she pulled on his arm and turned his body towards her again, and this time, she felt the kiss in every part of her body.

*

Charlie held her hand as they entered a taxi.

'One stop or two?' he whispered to her so the driver wouldn't hear them.

'One,' she said.

'Are you sure?'

'Yes,' she smiled at him. They sat there, her hand in his. His hand was soft, and his thumb carefully stroked hers. They looked out their windows, like they had been holding hands for years.

*

Charlie found his keys, opened the door, and let her enter. He turned on the dim lights. The scarf from earlier was gone. The house was warm, and the floor made a squeaking sound as she stepped inside. It was as if time was going slowly, every move felt like a part of a dance routine. She stepped out of one shoe at the time, descending onto the soft carpet. She let her coat slip off her shoulders, exposing her neck, and immediately he helped her getting her coat off her, slowly. She felt his breath on her neck, as if he wanted to kiss her, but didn't dare. She turned around and found herself a few inches away from his face. He was taller than her; her eyes met his chin.

'You seem tiny now,' he said, as he looked down at her. Christine felt unarmed and at ease, like her shoes had been heavy armour. For the first time, she could really take her time and smell him. Charlie didn't smell like a scent from a bottle, but the scent of him. It was indescribable, like nothing she had smelled before. She felt like this was the scent all male perfumes tried to copy. His bow tie was still hanging around his neck, and she looked at the unbuttoned shirt, and the chest underneath. Charlie just stood there, looking at her. He bit his lip. Christine was surprised that he was not as confident as she would imagine, as he did not dare to kiss her or touch her. She found it quite sweet that he seemed nervous.

'Would you like a glass of wine, maybe?' he finally said.

'Oh, the cheap plonk from the expensive cabinet?' They both started laughing.

'Maybe a glass and some water, if you wouldn't mind,'

Christine said. They walked downstairs, the light still dimmed .

'Some music, maybe? Any preferences?' Charlie was on his way to the display. Soon a smooth, deep voice was singing a Christmas song. 'Just because it is actually Christmas soon …' Charlie seemed to regret it as soon as it started. Charlie went to the kitchen island to pour some wine. Christine started singing along.

'Don't worry. I like it. A bit cliche, but anything you would put on would be up for a harsh critique. At least you're able to adapt your routine to the season.'

'My routine?' Charlie was looking at her, a bit blank. 'Is that really what you think of me?' Christine immediately felt she had stepped too far. She knew from his nerves earlier on, that for him, she was not just a random girl. Charlie was waiting for an answer, with two glasses ready to be filled in front of him. Christine approached him and jumped up to sit on the counter next to him. She was a bit afraid that he didn't approve and was glad when he didn't correct her. She looked directly into his eyes.

'Hey, I'm sorry.' Christine took a deep breath. 'This is a bit intimidating for me. Being one of the girls that you take with you home, give some wine and music, and forget the next day. I am happy to be here tonight, but I am not used to being one of those girls. So I make jokes. I'm sorry.' She searched Charlie's eyes for a smile. He leaned against the counter and looked down. 'I don't want to make you feel uncomfortable, or make you feel like you're doing something you don't really want to do. I don't want to be a mistake.'

Christine laid her hand over his. He looked up, and into her eyes.

'I really want to be here,' she said. He smiled at her, but still didn't dare to be closer to her face. He handed her a glass of wine. Charlie smiled. She moved her face nearer his.

'One thing is wrong though … I don't think I will ever forget you,' he whispered.

'Cheesy,' she whispered back right before they kissed. She unbuttoned a few more of his buttons, slowly. She then untied her shirt that she had borrowed from the bartender, and lifted her arms so he could pull it over her head. He was now standing between her legs. The top of her dress was around her waist, so he now saw her silk slip and the top of her bra. She kissed him again, her hands on his chest. She jumped down from the counter to be closer to him. She could feel him, although there were a lot of fabric between them. She smiled at him and wasn't nervous anymore.

'Do you want to go upstairs?' he suddenly said in a low voice.

'Yes.'

'Are you sure?'

'Yes. I have wanted this for a very long time, for years actually.' Charlie took her hand and held it all the way upstairs. He didn't say a word. Christine passed door after door on the way up, her toes sinking into the soft carpet on the steps. When they reached the top floor, she turned around so he could unzip the skirt of her dress. It fell down. She turned around and stepped out of all the fabric.

'Why didn't you just wear that tonight?' Charlie said as she stood there in a long silk slip with some tulle at the bottom to give the skirt some extra volume.

'It's an undergarment designed for the dress,' Christine said laughingly.

'No one could have guessed that. It just seems a lot more like you,' he said. Christine then let him pull down each strap.

Gown in a Paper Bag

Christine didn't open her eyes, although she was awake. She tucked the pillow under her face again and took a deep breath.

She sensed the smell of last night, the smell she couldn't describe. She felt the weight of an arm wrapped around her. It was nice, warm, and hairy. It wasn't Henrik's. Then she remembered everything. His tender kisses, his warm and toned body, the weight of it on her. His wet kiss on her neck and behind her ear. His smell. The taste of his lips. Her fingers through his thick hair. His brown eyes, how he had looked at her, and made sure she was feeling okay. How he had brushed her hair away from her face. How great his body made her feel, and now his warm body made a safe nook for her to lie in. It had been great. It *was* great. Except she knew *she* wasn't great. It wasn't great for her life.

Christine knew this moment would end very soon, and she would be filled with guilt. She knew almost for certain that Henrik had done this to her one time too many, but she couldn't really distinguish whether his cheating was a part of his illness or not. Christine felt like she didn't have an excuse. She knew why she had done this. She knew she was the one that had to end her relationship, and this would force her to do it. She knew that she could have stopped this, she knew she could have resisted it. She couldn't blame the alcohol, and she knew it wasn't revenge. Still, she was shocked by herself. Up until now, she had considered herself an honest and trustworthy person, and she did feel that she didn't really know that she'd had this in her.

She felt guilt for Charlie, because she knew for certain now that he had feelings for her. She had feelings for him as well, but what were they exactly? *Am I in love? Was it nice to get attention? Be looked at again?* It was so wrong, but yet it felt so right.

*

Christine opened her eyes and looked around. The bedroom wasn't that much different from last night, it was still airy and white. It was tidy, with a long wall covered in curtains. Last night she had thought the curtains were hiding his closet or a small TV room, but she understood now there was a big roof terrace behind them, since she could spot glass doors on each side with daylight flooding in. Her dress was neatly lying over a beautiful leather chair. Charlie must have put it there. She looked over to what then must be the way to the bathroom. She didn't want to look at him, because she knew that if she looked at him sleeping, she would fall for him, if she hadn't already. She slowly lifted his arm away from her. Christine collected her clothes, but before she went to the bathroom, she just couldn't resist taking a quick look at Charlie. His dark brown hair was all messed up, and his long lashes were perfect. His stubble made his chin look even more chiselled. His body was nicely tanned, but it seemed more like his natural skin tone than from a studio of some kind. She passed a perfect walk-in-closet with glass doors, and suits on wooden hangers inside. So his cabinets were tidy as well. At the end of the room, she could spot the bathroom. It had two big windows opening onto the street, and she could see the top of the trees. The windows were translucent, so no one could see in, but daylight filled the room. The bathroom floors and counter were in white marble, and she couldn't see any cabinets. One translucent glass door led into the shower, and she entered. Christine turned on the tap and tried to be very quick. As she peered out the door in search for a towel, she saw Charlie, who must have woken up from the sound of the shower. He grabbed a towel from a hidden cabinet, one to put around himself, and one for her. She stood there, with her head out of the shower, and smiled at him. He kissed her softly on the lips, but she withdrew quickly. Last night was over, and her guilt was overwhelming. She felt that she was disappointing him. He smiled understandingly but didn't give her the towel. Instead he held it out for her with both arms, so she would have to let him cover her in the towel. It felt so nice to be taken care of.

'I shouldn't have let you out of the bed,' he said as he gave her a hug.

'I have to go,' Christine whispered. She rushed out and lifted up a pair of jeans lying perfectly folded on a chair, and a belt lying on top. She looked at Charlie, and without a word he just nodded. On her way downstairs, she put on Charlie's jeans, her own heels, and she made a knot in the skirt of her silk slip so it wouldn't show under her coat. As she putting in her clothes, Charlie had put her massive gown into a black paper bag. He held it out to her. As she grabbed it, and said thank you, he grabbed her hand. She paused and turned to look straight into his big brown eyes. After a moment, he finally said:

'Are you sure you can't you stay?'

Christine couldn't look into his puppy eyes any longer and just shook her head. She was outside after a few seconds.

*

The sky was white like cotton that day, and there was a sense of where the sun was. Like the sky couldn't decide if it was a good day or not. She went back to the hotel and got straight into bed. She tried to cry, but she couldn't. She tried to think about Charlie, but she didn't know what to feel about him. She just felt numb. It was the first day in forever that she hadn't cried. After a while under the duvet, Christine heard a text come in. It was from Heidi.

'Looks like it was more than lunch ...'

Heidi had attached a link to her text, to an article in one of the gossip sites that she followed. The title said: "Henrik parties solo while his girlfriend gets cosy with finance wonder boy." Christine couldn't breathe. She skimmed through the article. Henrik was pictured with several blonde girls in Copenhagen. He was there by himself, and though no one else would notice, Christine noticed a darkness in his eyes. He wasn't smiling. Others might have said he got a sexy look, but Christine knew he was on his way into his darkness. Then, there were pictures of her. Pictures of her with Charlie walking yesterday, and then there were pictures of her *leaving this morning*! There was no question that it was her, in her heels, at Charlie's door, and her dress sticking out of a bag.

Christine continued to skim the article. '… while his girlfriend was in London cosying up to a hunky finance hotshot, one of London's most eligible bachelors. She visited his home, and it seemed a lot more than a business lunch.'

Christine replied to Heidi with one word: '*F****'

Christine knew that this was a nuclear bomb, and she had pushed the button. Although there had been a lot written about Henrik, nothing had been this revealing.

Another message from Heidi : **'Was his house amazing?'**

Christine laughed in-between her sobs. '**It was perfect in a nice but maybe creepy way. Nothing happened.'**

'**Nothing happened? Why not?**'

'**I need to end things with Henrik. Was just nice to get**

some attention for once.'

'Where are you? I tried calling you earlier. I'm onboard the plane already, they've closed the doors. If I had seen this article before, I would never have left you by yourself.'

'I must have been asleep, at the hotel. Will most likely stay in this room forever. How did your night go?'

'It was amazing, will tell you all about it later. Need to turn off my phone.'

Christine then continued to cry. She cried for the Henrik who she would never fix, for her relationship, she cried for her friendship with Heidi who she had lied to, but she cried mostly for herself. She felt awful and horrible, like the worst person in the world. Most of all, she felt sorry for being in the situation she found herself in. She just wanted to fall asleep. She hoped that when she woke up, several years would have passed, and this would all be over.

*

After a while, she woke up. Was it Sunday? Monday? She went for a walk. It was the same sky as before. She turned the corner and walked along the busy street, walking towards a green on the opposite side of the road. She passed a nursery school, and Christine could see a small boy being picked up by his mum. She had started to notice families a lot more lately. The boy was standing there with a red jacket and a stuffed white animal under his arm. Christine looked at the assistant in her pin-striped uniform. She saw a tattoo of a star sneaking out from under her sleeve, quite like the painting in the kitchen at home. Christine's eyes filled again with tears. Then they started to roll down her cheeks, without end. She wasn't just crying because Henrik was sick, again. This time, she knew she was crying because she knew it was over.

*

Christine stood before the entrance to her home. The old glass doors were thin, but the door felt so heavy to push open. She could smell old cigarettes, alcohol and stuffy, stale air, like time had stood still there since before she left for London. She went into the kitchen. The painting that she hated caught her eye. For the first time, she understood what Henrik had meant. She felt like the worst person in the world, and yet somehow, the painting told her that everyone had their secrets. Everyone had regrets and remorse that they just had to live with. She found Henrik by the dining table. He was leaning over the computer, with his headphones on.

'Hi,' she said.

He didn't respond. She waved her hand in front of his face.

He quickly looked at her, waved back, and then looked at his screen again. She took his headphones off.

'Listen to this! I think I just composed something great!' he said and handed her the headphones.

'Maybe I will listen later. Have you slept at all?'

'Listen to this,' he said, and put his headphones on her head. She had them on for a few seconds before she took them off. An intense beats laid on to off each other with a high pitch, was not music at all, and she got shivers down her spine. She pulled herself together, so he wouldn't see her in tears.

'Pretty great,' she lied.'I know.'

'Do you want to go for a drive? Maybe you'll get some sleep in the car?' He finally looked at her properly. His eyes were red, and he looked exhausted. 'Maybe that is a good idea.'

*

The winter sun made a magical appearance and turned the snow to crystals. Henrik sat there in the passenger seat. He hadn't said a word since they'd left the flat. Henrik turned to her.

'I think you're right. I need some sleep. What would I have done without you?'

'I will always take care of you,' Christine smiled, comforting at him.

'Why are you with me?'

'Because I care about you. That will never change.'

'You are always there for me, and you always take care of me. I am such a shitty boyfriend.'

Christine didn't deny it. 'It would be nice if you wanted to be with me when you were doing good as well.' Christine squeezed his hand, since she couldn't give him a hug.

'It's not a good thing, is it?'

'I can't just be your girlfriend when you are feeling down.'

'I know.'

Christine felt her phone ringing several times. She knew it was Charlie. It rung several times. Finally, it stopped.

*

After seven long days of several missed calls and texts, Christine finally gathered herself and started writing a response. She sat there on the edge of the bed. Even her bed didn't feel like it was hers to enjoy.

'Hi, I'm so sorry I haven't returned your calls. Henrik is sick, and I can't tell him now. I am truly sorry. Happy

Christmas.' She pressed send. She let her head land on the bed with the biggest bang a duvet could make.

Not a Walk in the Park

Christine heard the doorbell. She froze. She knew who it was. She had avoided him all week, and she had made sure she had packed all her stuff from the office before he would return. The week had been awful. Harald had had the most compassionate look on his face as she asked for unpaid leave for an uncertain amount of time, to figure her relationship and her life out. He asked if she and Henrik were over, but that was a question she couldn't answer, as she didn't know. Harald knew that it was very unlikely she would ever return to work. She had started crying, and he hadn't been able to hide his tears either. She had known Harald would be the most difficult one to tell, her relationship with Harald and Wenche was one of the things she didn't want to loose from the relationship with Henrik. Her whole life was based on the life she shared with Henrik, and now it was all falling apart. Harald had, of course, called Wenche immediately after Christine had stopped by his office. Wenche then sent Christine a message a few minutes after, and asked if she could stop by later on. When Wenche came later that evening, Christine had opened the door, and they had just hugged. They hugged for a very long time, and there were floods of tears. Finally, Wenche had said:

'I understand. I understand. We know he hasn't been there for you for a very long time. No matter what the two of you decide to do, you are still my adoptive daughter.' When she had called her own parents, they said they had been expecting trouble for years, and they would help her through it all, whatever she and Henrik decided to do. Her mother had asked if she wanted to come home for a while. But since Henrik was away anyway, she might as well stay in the apartment for a while, until she figured everything out. Everyone around her sort of knew that the actual breakup with Henrik would be inevitable, and finally she also knew that it was very unlikely there was any relationship to save. Christine knew she needed time to think. She needed to figure out what she wanted, but she also needed help to figure out how she could help Henrik. She was not able to give it all up just yet, although she knew it was extremely fragile. She knew *he* was extremely fragile.

Then there was Charlie. She knew it was him at the door. She had checked his calendar, and knew he would be in Oslo. He was the part of this mess that she had no idea how to handle. He was the one she wanted to be without, but he was the part she couldn't get out of her mind. That night was still locked into her memory, but it was more like an intense dream than a real-life experience.

She couldn't stop thing about how good it was, and that made her feel so awful. She felt sick when she thought about it, and therefore tried not to think about it at all. That was how she wanted to treat it as well, like it didn't happen. She knew why she had done it, but it shocked her that she wasn't filled with guilt while it lasted, when she felt so unimaginably awful now. She had to make her own life work, and maybe Henrik was in it in some way, but most likely he wasn't if he wanted to live the life he had up until now. Christine froze of the thought that she'd had to sleep with Charlie to force herself to do this. She wasn't sure whether the affair was a necessary event, though it was highly regretful.

The media had certainly also catapulted this further and faster than she ever could fathom. The article of her and Charlie's walk in the park and her leaving his house was stuck in her mind. She knew there weren't any pictures of them in his bed, but there might as well have been. Of course everyone knew that she had slept with him.

And now he was at her door. She hadn't replied any texts except the one yesterday where she brutally dumped him. If he was ever actually interested in more, Christine didn't know, and she didn't want to know. She didn't want to see him at all, but she knew he wouldn't stop contacting her until she saw him. She wouldn't buzz him in, as she knew she wouldn't get him to leave.

It also felt very personal to let him into her home, and she wanted to keep him at a distance. She therefore put on her coat and went down the stairs to the front door, while the buzzer rang several times.

Christine carefully opened the door. There, a few steps below her, he stood. He was looking at her with his big brown eyes, seeming surprised that something happened.

'Hi,' Charlie said quietly.

Christine didn't say anything, and she didn't smile. She just gave him a stressed look.

'Can we please go for a walk and talk?'

She looked to the ground. Then she looked at him, and quickly shook her head. She was already freezing and wrapped her arms around herself.

'You won't return my calls.'

She was still silent.

'You're not going to say anything to me?' He gave her a piercing stare. Then, he walked up two steps to be closer to her. She took a deep breath and looked down the street. "I don't know what to say. What do you want from me, Charlie? You want me to leave him for you? I've barely met you without your dinner jacket on. I can't leave my life for someone I've only met when I have a glass of champagne in my hand. It's not real ... I can't just be with Henrik, and the next second be with you.'

'That night meant something to me, and I thought it did for you as well."

She didn't answer, she just looked down.

'The thing is, every time I've seen you, I sort of hope that you won't be there. That there is no longer a reason for you to meet me, that you've broken up with Henrik, and that you have quit work. So every time I see you, although my heart skips a beat, my heart also sinks. I feel like I lose. I thought we were about to change that.'

Christine looked to the ground.

Charlie continued: 'Seriously Christine, is this really the guy you're marrying? What you chose in life? You're staying with him? I know you don't care about the money, so is it out of guilt? I get that you don't want to hurt him while he is down, but this is *your* life, Christine.'

She finally looked at him. She was shaking, and as she started speaking, her voice was too.

'Henrik and I have shared so much and have a life together.

Things are not always great, he's not here all the time. But it's not like you live down the street either. You have no idea what it is like for him here. You don't share your life with me, you don't know how it is. Henrik is sick, and of all people, you know. How can you expect me to leave him like this? I can't leave him just like that. I never should have led you on. Maybe Henrik and I decide down the road to part ways, but right now, I can't have any contact with you. I need to sort myself out. I am sorry my moment of misjudgement dragged you into this.'

A long pause came.

'I was your drunken mistake, then.' Charlie no longer tried to look her in the eyes. Christine sighed. She didn't mean to offend him, but she didn't have the energy to correct it. What was the point, anyway? Now he would at least leave her alone, although she felt even worse.

'What's there to say? It was what it was, but that was it.'

'I was wrong then,' he took a step back, 'to think there was something more.'

Christine couldn't stand to be there any longer. She felt her eyes filling up with tears, and she knew they wouldn't be silent either. She turned around quickly and got inside right before her sobbing began. She had these breakdowns these days, and she was surprised that she still didn't know how to control them. She ran towards the kitchen window, where she could see the front door if she pressed her nose to it. Charlie was still there, but now he was sitting on her steps with his head in his hands. *What did I just do?* Instead of having another breakdown, she felt blank. She looked down the street. It was so quiet. If anyone was outside, they would have heard their argument. Christine felt embarrassed, that she hadn't had any control of her emotions or her voice. She looked a little further down the street and she saw two guys sitting in a car, with what looked like some black things in the front window. Christine gasped. *Are they photographers?* Christine pulled her head back quickly, and ran to her bedroom, jumped in her bed, and covered herself with her duvet.

*

It didn't help at all. She knew the duvet couldn't cover her mistakes.

The Deal Breaker

'After lunch today, do can you think you could maybe drive me to the airport?' Henrik didn't even look at Christine while asking. He kept staring at his phone. Christine was in the bathroom with the door open, in case Henrik wanted to join her in the shower like he used to.

'What? You're leaving? Now?' Her answer got extra volume from the acoustics in the bathroom.

'Yeah, I have to. They're all waiting for me. The set only took a short break.' Christine walked to the bedroom again, completely naked. She was hoping he would notice her. 'Do you think you are well enough to just go back like that?' Her voice was mild and calm. Henrik's gaze had not left his phone. He was mumbling.

'I just had to sleep a bit. I don't get well until I get out of this place. This place is depressing, you know.'

Christine looked down at the floor, not knowing what to say. She wanted to cover herself up, but instead of going back to the bathroom, she replied, 'Well, it's our home.' Henrik looked up as Christine was biting her lip, trying to hold back her tears. 'I didn't mean it like that.'

'Can I come?' she asked, knowing the answer. He didn't reply, just kept swiping something on his screen.

'We've been over this. You know it's just work, and it's no fun for you to be there.'

'I don't care whether it's fun or not, I just want to see you every day, at least for a while.'

'It's not so easy for me to have you there while I'm working. I don't want to feel like I have a babysitter or nurse with me.'

It then became quiet. Henrik head was still bent over his phone.

'I'm actually your girlfriend,' Christine said in a low voice, so Henrik couldn't hear. She walked back to the bathroom to grab a towel.

*

'Call me when you get there,' Christine said as she stopped the car.

'What would I ever do without you?' Henrik smiled at her and gave her a kiss on her forehead.

'It would be nice if you wanted to see me when you are not feeling bad as well.'

Henrik ignored her words. They both stepped out of the car. Henrik kissed her head again and tossed his big bag over his shoulder.

'Call you later, then, I guess,' he said as he walked off. Christine stood there, watching Henrik walk into the airport entrance. She felt completely empty. They hadn't discussed what the whole world knew, the pictures everyone had seen. She didn't know if he knew, if he even cared. *When was the last time he looked me in the eyes?* She watched the other families dropping loved ones off on Christmas Day. People smiling to each other, talking to each other, people caring for each other. *How do we look to the outside world? Like a couple, or as siblings? Can people tell that there is nothing left between us?*

All of a sudden, she thought she saw a familiar figure infront of a car a bit further ahead. Was it *Alex*? She could feel the heat starting to rise towards the top of her head. She knew it had to be him, it had to be him that had tipped the media off in London. As she was on her way to speak to him, she could hear a whistle and Henrik calling her name. She turned towards the entrance again.

'Happy New Year!' Henrik shouted. She waved, but didn't know how to smile. She watched Henrik go through the doors before she ran towards the other car. As she approached it, she was certain it was him. His short arms and full figure, his hair so sleek she wondered if it could all be lifted off like a plastic hair piece.

"Hi," she said as she tapped Alex's shoulder.

'Well, Merry Christmas, Christine!' Alex leaned in to give her a hug, but he must have felt Christine's icy demeanour already.

'Wow, what's with the mad face?' Alex joked. Christine didn't find at amusing at all, but tried to relax.

'I know you and Henrik haven't always been the best of friends, but calling paparazzi and suggesting I am having an affair with my boss is a bit of a low blow, now isn't it?'

Alex took a moment, and then started laughing.

'Although I have indeed been enjoying reading a certain type of news lately, I am very sorry to disappoint you, but calling paparazzi is well below my standards. Not only do I make more than enough money on my own, tipping the press? It can't be much, what the press would pay for that news.'

Christine looked at him surprised. She knew that Alex wouldn't lie about his triumphs, so she knew he spoke the truth.

'But we met you just minutes before the first pictures were taken. I don't understand.'

'Weird coincidence, I know. But it wasn't me. It's not like Henrik *cares* what you do. I hasn't annoyed him to flirt with you for years.'

Christine stood there, silenced. As always, Alex's frankness was beyond what anything imaginable. He continued: 'You should ask yourself, "*who* else was there?" I do not gain anything from seeing you cheating on Henrik, but you should ask yourself, "who *would* gain a fortune?"'

'I don't quite follow …' Christine said, blank to any other suspicions.

'Your darling *boss*,' Alex said slowly.

'What do you mean?'

'Who just quit his job days ago?'

'Charlie.' Christine said quickly. 'And me, of course.'

'Correct. Now, do you remember a particular rumour about a Californian tech company that was after him? The rumour is that they have doubled or even *tripled* their offer, most likely so high, he can't refuse. There would only be one tiny problem, his sign-on bonus with Harald would still be locked for serveral years. The only way he could get both his money and a quick exit is if Harald had some reason to fire him, but not because of his performance. Do I need to fill in the rest for you as well?'

Christine was still confused.

'I see you still need further explanation. Charlie needed to get out of his contract immediately. The salary and sign-on fee for his new job is rumoured to be insanely high, no one could ever pass it up. But still, you just don't give up on a large sum of money from your current job, in Charlie's case, that is at Harald's. Those who have *a lot* tend to want *more*. Performing badly would leave Charlie with nothing, and embezzlement would leave him with nothing, and he would even be prosecuted, and lose the new job too. He needed to do something they couldn't legally hang him for, but was still so bad Harald would want to get rid of him, but in a way that meant he couldn't deny him his bonus. Do you follow?'

Christine nodded.

'So, a very public and humiliating affair with Harald's daughter-in-law was a pretty safe way to get out of his contract, without actually committing a felony, or his professional reputation. This one hit close to home, especially since Harald would care more about your infidelity than Henrik would. You know, being from a generation where they only expect men to be cheating. And you, I am sad to say, well, you are collateral damage.'

Christine felt her legs disappear beneath her. She couldn't breathe. *Is this true? Could I have been used to get out of a contract?* Charlie had left his job a few days after her, and of course all statements were extremely polite and completely controlled by their communications department. *Could Charlie have been lying to me this entire time? Had he seized a possibility to use my bad relationship for his own good?* Christine didn't know what to say. She felt confused, and she was getting nauseous.

'Look, Christine. I know you have a kind heart, but it's a selfish and cruel world you've tangled yourself in. It was cold but clever, I have to give him that. I am quite impressed actually, even I couldn't have thought of that one. But hey, maybe eventually you'll realise this might be good for you. I have always through you were too good for Henrik, anyway.'

Christine didn't reply.

'Merry Christmas,' Alex said, and smiled. He turned around and started walking back to his car. His smile had felt genuine, and he didn't say goodbye in a smug way. It was almost like he had some compassion for her right now.   Christine stood there for a while before she walked back to her car. She took a deep breath but didn't turn the engine on just yet. She grabbed her phone and started writing a list of things to do:

New job

New place

Break up

Three simple lines, but *oh* so big.

The Fourth Year

The Postcard

Christine was looking at herself in the mirror. Her makeup was all done, her hair was flowing in large, shiny waves. She was standing there in a navy-blue silk dress. It was simple and elegant. She smiled at herself. She remembered what she had felt like the previous few years, but this time was the first time she liked what she saw. The horrible feeling of being the worlds worst person had finally started to fade. The horrible freezing feeling down her back only appeared maybe once a day now. The room she stood in was white and bright, and she picked up her coat from the oak bench in the hallway. At the table next to the bench, she glanced at a postcard lying there. It was stamped from somewhere in Mexico.

Greetings from Mexico! I am actually starting to like this new version of 'us'. You've always been my best friend, and I realise I haven't lost that. Your bestie, H.

She put the postcard in the bowl with all the others. Before she went out the door, she picked up her phone and wrote.

On my way to your parent's dinner, give me a ring later this weekend if you want to catch up. I hope you are having the time of your life. Bestie C.

The doorbell rang.

'Hi! Just come up, drinks are ready!'

The Return of the Shawl

'I've missed you terribly. See you at our place for brunch on Sunday?' Wenche gave her kisses on both cheeks when she entered the party.

'I would love to.' Christine smiled before she had to move on to give Harald a kiss as well. She knew that this moment would be scrutinised and the camera flashes would go off more than usual, now that she and Henrik was not together any more. The last year had been so hard but good for them both. They had spoken almost every day for the first few months, cried a lot, and through the distance they had managed to transition into just close friends, like they were siblings, who knew that their upbringing together would always be attached somehow. Strangely, without the obligations that being a couple required, they had managed to support each other. Christine turned around to look at Heidi and Eric, who were entering behind her, who had both said she could come and interrupt them at any time. It was so sweet that they had also met her for a drink before, as Christine now longer would attend the Oslo pre-drinks. She had prepared with Heidi how she should reply comments about the break-up. It was so comforting to have them both as a safe harbour for the party she dreaded, but Christine knew she had to show everyone that she was on good terms with Henrik and his family. There were of course some people she dreaded to meet more than others, including Alex. Unexpectedly, she ran into Kristian at the cloakroom queue.

'Long time, no see!' he said as he approached her. 'I hope you are doing well, and that you have managed to get through all this.' Christine gave him a kiss on each cheek. 'Yes, I am doing well, actually. It has just been so much, the new job, the new place, and everything. But I feel like I am finally getting everything sorted.'

'Well, the media is still very much interested in how you are doing. We could hear it all the way in here that it was you who were arriving.'

'The weird thing is, I am completely comfortable with it now, because I know they will eventually not care anymore.'

'Well, at least Harald and Wenche still love you, and the

media can't make a good story out of that one. I think everyone is sort of tired of reading about your break-up anyway. Henrik's life is far more interesting than yours. You never crossed me as a person who wanted that attention.'

Christine smiled at Kristian.

'Do you know he is here?' Kristian said.

'Who?' Christine said, surprised. She knew Henrik was away, so she knew Kristian wasn't referring to him.

'Over there,' Kristian nodded in the direction of the big windows. Christine recognised him without seeing his face, the way his hair was always perfectly cut in the back, though the lengths of his almost-black mane varied. His dinner jacket was better fitted than anyone else's. She could see his charming smile as a reflection in the windows. He was speaking to a group of people from the office, but beside him was this girl from the London office. She usually wasn't present at the event in Oslo. *Is he really here? Did he have no shame at all?*

It was like he knew he was been watched, because he all of a sudden turned and looked Christine right in the eyes. Startled, Christine turned to Kristian.

'And he even brought a girl!I can't remember her name, but hasn't she been drooling all over him for years?' Christine hid her mouth behind a glass of champagne so Charlie couldn't read her lips, in case he knew how. Christine felt the girl was the complete opposite of her. She was more like Heidi, tiny, blonde, and no one expected her ever to say something clever. She was wearing the shawl she had noticed at Charlie's last year.

'Since Charlie is here, he and Harald must have parted amicably. You know, I don't want to get into what really happened between the two of you, but I have to say, you and Charlie strike me as much better match than you and Henrik. Henrik didn't deserve you.'

'The rest of the country doesn't agree with you on that one.'

'Those who know you, know the truth. Henrik had the chance with you, and everyone knows he blew it. If you did end up with Charlie, no one would blame you, you know.'

'Well, I see I am not the only one who has been fooled by his charm.'

Kristian looked at her strangely.

'All I know is that Charlie was really into you, everyone could see that.'

Christine didn't answer.

'Oh, he's coming over. Get ready.' Kristian exclaimed.

Christine could now see Charlie out of the corner of her eye, approaching her. *Does he really want to speak with me? Can't we just avoid each other all night like regular one-night-stands, instead of everyone looking at us right now, analysing every movement?*

'Kristian, it's always a pleasure running into you,' Charlie said as he shook Kristian's hand.

'Likewise, Charlie,' Kristian managed to squeeze in, before Charlie stressfully continued to Christine.

'Lovely seeing you, Miss Loveness. I thought you were banned from this thing,' he said as he kissed her cheek.

'Likewise, Charlie,' Christine quickly replied, in a sharp, tense voice. The girl appeared right behind Charlie. 'I believe you both know my date'" he said.

'Yes, we do. What a pleasure seeing you again, Jenny,' Kristian replied for them both, with an emphasis on the name that he had just remembered.

'So, how's California, Charlie?' Christine continued the tense conversation.

'I wouldn't know.' Charlie looked at her surprised.

'I thought you started working for a tech firm in Silicon

Valley.'

'No. Actually, I've started my own technology company, based in London, mostly.' It was not the answer Christine was expecting at all.

'Oh, well, I do hope it is going well,' she said more lightly, at the same time as millions of thoughts went through her head. *Was the rumours not true? If the California job doesn't exist, what else was not true about the story Alex told me? The story has to be true, why else would she be interested in me?*

'It's going according to the plan, but we do need more founding soon.'

'Hmm,' Christine was still not convinced. 'You are probably good at that, earning people's trust, for your own benefit.'

'What?' Charlie quickly replied and looked confused. Before Christine could to answer, Alex suddenly cut into the conversation.

'Who is this amazingly beautiful lady you've have by your side?' he said, clearly referring to Jenny, who he could not take his eyes off.

'Oh, you haven't met before? Alex, this is Jenny, Jenny this is Alex,' Charlie said quickly, not interested in giving them any further introduction. Christine seized the opportunity to slowly drift away from the conversation, when all of a sudden, she had Charlie in front of her.

'What did you mean by that comment?' he asked with a tense voice.

'Oh you know perfectly well what I mean. Is that why you are here again, to squeeze more money out of Harald? I understand why he invited you, so it wouldn't appear that there was anything dramatic regarding your resignation, but it's disappointing to see you will use it for your own benefit, again,' Christine answered in a nice voice, as she was trying to not make a scene.

'Well, I guess I can say the same for you.' Charlie on the other hand wasn't trying to hide his anger, although she didn't understand what he meant by his response. The dinner bell rang.

'Saved by the bell, I guess. Well, that was pleasant. Have a splendid evening, then.' Christine started to walk to the dining room.

'Likewise,' Charlie said with an intense gaze. Heidi was suddenly behind Christine. 'That was some feisty behaviour, Christine. Be careful not to make a scene, I thought you were done with creating gossip and chit chat. Meet me at the entrance bar after the first course?'

'Sure.' Christine knew that she had to finally reveal to Heidi the whole story with Charlie. She still felt bad for sleeping with him when she knew Heidi liked him. It felt as though she had betrayed Heidi, although Heidi had met her now-boyfriend that fateful night last year.

*

'What was that even about? I don't think I have ever heard you being so harsh with anyone before. That was not a very typical behaviour from you, and with Charlie, who was so into you?'

'I haven't been completely honest with you, Heidi. I didn't sleep over at Charlie's because I couldn't get a hold of Henrik. I feel so bad, I had a thing with him, when I knew you liked him.'

'Really? I didn't tell you then, but I secretly wanted you to be with Charlie instead of Henrik!'

'Ha, right,' Christine said ironically.

'No, I am serious!'

'Didn't you like him though?'

'No, he told me the first time I met him that he was stunned the first time he met *you*. I've tried to set you up with him ever since.'

Christine sighed: "Well, long story short. I did something

stupid when breaking up with Henrik. I guess I needed an excuse to actually end it, and I thought I was falling for Charlie. He was really sweet, and I slept with him after the dinner last year. Then, I found out he tipped the media so that Harald would find out he was having an affair with his future daughter in law, and release him from his contract. He made millions getting out of his contract quickly.'

'Hmm. That was a lot of information. We'll get back to all the nitty-gritty details later, but most importantly right now: Charlie did really, *really* like you, I know that for sure, and he works in *London,* not Silicon Valley.'

'Yes, that London thing didn't completely add up,' Christine admitted. 'The Silicon Valley sign-on-fee might not be a part of the story then. There surely must have been another advantage to get out of the deal with Harald quickly. Why else would he tip off the media?'

'Are you sure it was him, though?' Heidi asked.

'No one else knew we were together that day, besides him. No one knew of both a walk in the park in London, and us being together at my door in Oslo.'

'Well, if they knew you were in the park, they could have followed you.'

The bell rang again. They had to continue their conversation afterwards. As Christine took her seat at the table, she could hear her phone vibrate in her bag. She knew it was not appropriate at all, but today, she couldn't resist. She suspected this was something more interesting than the daily text from her mum. Since the others around the table weren't seated yet, she opened her bag carefully under the table, and quickly turned down the screen light on her phone. It was a text from Heidi.

I have to tell you something. You have to know that I did it with all the best intentions.

Christine looked over at Heidi, who was looking down at her phone, obviously not daring to look at Christine. A new text came:

I almost knew for certain that Henrik was cheating on you, because I had heard rumours for so many years. And, since he always pinched my butt when he had been drinking, I knew he had no control when he was drunk. You always assumed the best of him, and I didn't have any solid proof. So, I did something I am not proud of, but I felt you needed help to get out of it all.

Their eyes quickly met, before Heidi continued writing. It took a few seconds before the next message appeared.

I was the one who tipped off the press about which hotel Henrik was staying at with Chloe. I did it again when I accidentally passed you and Charlie walking in a taxi, thinking maybe Henrik would leave you instead. I should never have called them, but I thought you would never leave Henrik if you didn't get a proper push. You are too kind to leave someone, especially if they're not well. But I really didn't mean for it to go as far as it did. I did not call them about you staying over, nor about Charlie on your steps in Oslo. But they must have known by then it was worth waiting outside, since it was already a money-making story. So it wasn't Charlie at all, it was actually me. Please forgive me.

Christine didn't answer. She was stunned. She felt like she was spinning around. Had she not listened to her best friend at all for these last years? She guessed if anyone knew her well, it was Heidi, and of course Heidi knew her relationship with Henrik was not a relationship to keep. Christine could not decide if she was mad at Heidi or not. Maybe if Heidi had told her a year ago, she would have been furious. But now, she knew all that had happened was for the better.

Another text came in.

Please, please forgive me. You should know that I haven't slept a whole night through for a year, regretting what I

started.

A second message came.

How mad are you? 1. You never want to speak to me ever again. 2. You want to slap me. 3. You are pissed off and need some time to think. 4. The fact that I haven't had a good night's sleep for a year has been punishment enough.

Christine quickly replied: **3**

She then looked at Heidi, who looked like she was trying her best to keep tears from running down her cheeks. Christine then sent another text.

Maybe 4

They looked at each other, and through her smile, Heidi's tears started running. She then wrote another text.

Charlie had and probably still has a massive crush on you. I am certain he only brought that airhead tonight to make you jealous.

Christine looked over at Charlie. *Had he been the good guy all along? Had he just wanted to be with me? How could I have turned a blind eye to Henrik over and over, and then be so judgemental towards Charlie?* She had known Henrik almost all her life, and she of course knew he wasn't a saint, but how could she assume Charlie would be that cruel? Of course, people in finance never said no to large sums of money, but believing he would pretend to be so into her to get out of his contract was on another level of cynicism.

*

She looked at him for a while, but he was looking nowhere close to her at all. She had forgotten how incredibly handsome she found him, and the memories from that night came back to her. Christine wrote a message Heidi, and told herself it was the last one, she would not be remembered for texting all night.

Meet me in the ladies after next course?

Of course.

When Christine got up to go to the ladies, she could see that Heidi had already left.

'What took you so long?' Heidi almost shouted at her when she arrived downstairs. 'I'm so sorry for making you a paparazzi target last year.'

'It's okay, Heidi,' Christine said. 'I know now that Henrik and I were together a lot longer than we should have been, but I was the last one to see it. I was by myself in that relationship the last few years. I'm sorry I wasn't honest with you about Charlie. I was embarrassed because I thought you liked him.'

'I did. For like *five minutes*, before he asked me to help him get *your* attention. How mad are you at me?'

'I am not mad at all. I am madder at myself that I had to create such a mess before I managed to think clearly.'

'Maybe you think clearly about Charlie as well now?'

'I guess I owe him an apology at least.'

'Go! Kiss and make up!'

'He's here with a date, remember? And maybe I just liked him last year because he was giving me the attention Henrik wasn't.'

'Well, be with him while you find that out then!'

Christine gave her a nervous look and went back to her seat. She watched Charlie through the whole dinner, and he didn't look at her once, not even in her direction. She tried to make interesting conversation with the people at her table, but her mind was not present at all. All she could think about was Charlie.

*

When the dinner was over, Christine got herself together and prepared to go up to him. She had a large sip of her wine before she approached him at the bar. He was talking to Kristian, and she felt comfortable that it was a conversations she was welcome by

Kristian to interrupt. She leaned in towards them, and although Kristian gave her smile as a confirmation of her presence, Charlie ignored her and didn't stop his story.

Finally, he said rudely, 'Can we help you with anything, Miss Loveness?'

'Actually, yes, can I have a word with you, Charlie? Kristian, would you excuse us for a moment?'

Charlie looked at Kristian.

'I could never say no to her,' Kristian said cheeky to Charlie. Charlie went towards the end of the bar. Christine thought there were too many people there and needed it to be more private.

'Would you mind terribly if we went outside?'

Charlie set down his glass and started walking out to the balcony.

'Would you like your coat?' She was getting nervous. She picked up the coats for both of them, while he waited by the door. When she arrived, he walked in front of her, but provocatively didn't hold up the door for her. He took a few steps outside, obviously wanting to stay close to the door, and after he put on his coat, he crossed his arms. Christine tried to look him in the eyes, but he avoided her gaze.

So she started: 'I guess I owe you an apology, for so many things.'

Charlie's face started to relax, and he dared to look at her.

'I know I was not being very nice to you last year. It was a shitty thing to just avoid you instead of speaking to you. I was also very rude to you earlier today, and now I'll explain to you the reason why.'

Charlie was looking towards the door: 'It's freezing, can you speed it up a bit?'

'After I spent the night at your place, I heard a rumour about you, which I sadly believed to be the truth. You see, the rumour was that you needed to get out of your contract in order to accept an offer from a Silicone Valley based tech firm, the one I was referring to earlier. The rumour said that the reason you slept with me and then tipped the press was because it was a way of quickly getting out of the contract with Harald, and still getting your bonus, as well as the massive sign-on fee for the Silicon Valley tech company. And I, not being in a very good place, and with low self-esteem, believed that there was no way on earth you would actually be into me. So, the rumour made sense to me at that point.'

Charlie looked frustrated and mad. 'Who told you that insane story?'

'Alex,' Christine said in a low voice.

'Alex?' Charlie was almost shouting.

Christine wrinkled her nose. She knew now how stupid it was to listen to Alex.

'What do you know about my contract? Has Harald told you anything? Anything at all about my departure?'

'No.' Christine was looking at the ground, not daring to see how mad Charlie was.

'Well, I must inform you that you are wrong about all those statements.'

'I know that now. I know that you did not tip the press.'

"I did not tip off the press, I did not get a bonus, I did not sign on to another job, and I certainly did *not* sleep with you to get out of a contract. I guess I now know how *little* you think of me. I am glad you have realised that I am not that type of person. So I guess all I can say is that your apology is accepted,' Charlie said coldly. He then took a deep breath, turned around, and walked inside. Christine looked around. A few smokers were quite far away from them, so she dared to raise her voice to stop him.

'That's it?' She followed him. When he grabbed the door, he

turned around and looked at her.

'You wanted to apologise, I guess you did, and I accepted. Now, will you excuse me, but I was in the middle of a conversation I would like to go back to.' Christine was confused. She hadn't thought about what would happen next, she had just thought about what she should say. She went back to her table and grabbed her glass. She then took up her phone, and went out on the balcony, pretending to make a phone call, needing a few minutes to gather her thoughts.

What did I expected would happen? That he would be all over me, kissing me passionately? He hasn't heard from me in a year. He is here with a girl, who's shawl I saw at his house. For all I know, they could have been going out for at least a year. Maybe I was his mistake at the beginning of their relationship, and he is now in love with this Jenny.

All of a sudden, Harald was by her side.

'So, my darling Christine, how are you?'

'I am not doing great. Not a good year, really.'

'You really like him, huh?'

'Who?'

'Don't you think I know? Of course, I knew even before

Charlie came and told me last year.'

'I didn't know how much I liked him until now, I guess,' Christine said.

'Christine, of course you know how much I would have wanted you to marry my son, but I would be the first one to say that he didn't deserve you. Charlie, on the other hand, well, I think he knows how to treat you well.'

'I think I am too late there. He doesn't want me now.'

'Let me tell you something, Christine. The Charlie who sat in my office before Christmas last year, he was pretty smitten. He wanted to leave his position, so he wouldn't be your boss, and he wouldn't be attached to me, or Henrik for that matter. I asked him, "*what if Christine doesn't want to be with you after all?*" He knew that seeing you, and hearing about you, would be uncomfortable for him, because then he would struggle to forget about you.'

'That's sweet to know at least.'

'Christine, a man does not sit in front of another man and tell him he has just a little crush. A sensible man does not leave a great job so a small infatuation can have her freedom. Only a man in love does that.'

'I though he'd had an affair with me to get out of his position without loosing a bonus.'

'Oh. That's not correct at all.'

'I know that now. I have apologised for that tonight. He accepted, and then he wasn't that interested in speaking to me any more.'

'Well, then you have certainly made a declaration of love!' Harald said sarcastically. 'Come on, Christine, the man left his job for you, that's how deeply in love he was, and all you can say is "I am sorry I thought you used me?" The more he felt rejected, the more persuasion he needs now, Christine. I will say he was REJECTED with a capital letters. Also, he didn't want his last bonus and salary. He said I should give it to you instead, that you were underpaid the years you worked for us. I think I have forgotten to give you that.'

Christine smiled. It was sort of nice to have a chat with Harald. He wasn't her dad, but he was pretty close.

She looked to the bar, where she knew Charlie was, now speaking to a colleague from the Oslo office. She watched him carefully, and finally, he was on his way to the bathroom. She followed him.

'Can I have a word with you again?' she asked carefully.

He sighed and turned around to go outside.

'Do you want your coat again?' she asked.

'That won't be necessary.'

Christine felt her nerves getting to her, and she was shaking even before she got outside. A group of guests passed them as they walked outside. Then they were alone. Christine felt blue from freezing.

'So, I was wondering if you had thought about my apology?'

Before she got any further, Charlie interrupted her. 'You know, I am so mad at you for even thinking I was the one tipping the media off. I have walked around for a year wondering if I had completely misinterpreted the situation, you just cut me completely off.'

Christine tried to get a word in. 'I was so confused, and not able to think straight at all in the middle of my break-up with Henrik.'

'I get that you had to sort things out, but to just *cut me off* like that, saying it meant *nothing*, was just so cruel. And now I learn that you thought that I would use you, and in cold blood broadcast that you were a cheater in the media? How could you think of me as such a villain? How could you even imagine that about me?' He was on his way inside. Then in anger he turned to her again and continued.

'What makes me *really* mad, is that you didn't even have the decency to confront me about it, you just went along and listened to Alex instead. *Alex*! I am furious at you for not telling me before today, when I have kept my mouth closed about everything. When you should have dumped Henrik years ago, I listened. When you ruthlessly slept with me, when you knew very well I was crazy about you and then wouldn't return my calls, I still told no one. Now it's been almost a year, and what disappoints me the most, is that not once have you thought maybe you shouldn't listen to Alex? Is your gut instinct so out of whack that you choose to listen to Alex instead of just asking me?'

'I *am* sorry,' began Christine. 'I am *so* sorry. I didn't know who to trust! It was just too much for me at the time, and I am sorry I didn't trust you or ask you about everything I heard.'

'Well, you should have. Now, will you please have the decency to leave me alone?'

'Well, I don't feel completely done with this.'

'No, Christine, we were done with this a year ago. Correction, *you* were done with this a *year* ago. Now, I know that relationships might not mean much to you, Christine, but I am actually here on a date, and I like to treat my girlfriend with respect, which I haven't really done tonight, with all interruptions from you.'

'Oh,' Christine said. "That was a bit of a low blow, Charlie. I tried to make a relationship work for a really long time, and you know that. I feel awful enough for what I did, but I liked you a lot too, you know. Let me get that straight. I *like* you, a *lot*, actually. I have liked you for a long time, I was just in the middle of ending a very long relationship, and I needed to be done with that. I am sorry I didn't end things sooner so I didn't spoil everything with you. I am sorry I was not able to separate right from wrong at the time." Christine didn't once take her eyes of Charlie.

'Okay,' he said, and walked inside. Christine stood there, and her eyes started to fill up with tears. *Was that it?* She had realised that Charlie was, most likely, the man of her dreams tonight, and she just found out she ruined every chance of being with him a year ago.

*

She walked inside, and quickly got her coat. She didn't let anyone meet her eyes, as she was struggling to hold back the tears from running down her face. She went outside and ordered a taxi as she walked down the street to the main gate. At the bottom of the slope, she could see two people kissing passionately, and then walking towards a taxi. *Is that Alex? Can someone possibly be charmed by him?*

*

Her taxi arrived shortly after. As she sat there and looked out the window down at the beautiful lit harbour front, she finally let her tears go. She cried for everything. She cried for her and Henrik, of what they never became, and she cried for Charlie, because she knew she could have been with him what she and Henrik never were. The taxi driver looked at her in the rear-view mirror.

'The tunnel over Skøyen or through the city, miss?'

'I know the tunnel is the shortest in terms of minutes, but I think I would like to drive through town tonight.'

Throughout the whole drive, she looked out the window. Streetlights and shop windows were lighting up the dark December night. There were lots of people outside, hurrying to the next bar or Christmas party. As they drove up Drammensveien, the street were empty again. She felt completely alone in the city, although she was safe and warm in a taxi. Over Solli plass there were loads of people trying to get to busses or trams, and she could watch the chaos from her little bubble. Then, as they drove up *Bygdøy Allé*, the streets were empty again.

'You can just stop here, I'll walk the rest,' Christine said to the driver. 'Thanks for a peaceful ride.'

He smiled at her.

'Good luck with the rest of your night,' she laughed, knowing he would have a lot of rather intoxicated passengers for the rest of the night. The cold started biting her cheeks the moment she stepped outside. She looked around, and she was all alone. Just her and the beautiful facades that kept her company.

The Common English Name

Christine started walking down the hill to her new flat, when she realised that Charlie was probably staying at Gabels Hus, where he always used to stay. *Maybe I should just sit there for a drink, in case he was returning from the party quite soon? It is rather desperate, but he turned up on my doorstep last year. If he is now the fantastic man that I first thought, there's no point in just giving up and going home.* Christine knew now that she had to work hard to at least manage to be friends with Charlie again. If they could at least be friends again, then maybe, in a while, they could try and be *more* than that. She would give him four years of friendship and waiting like he had done for her.

*

She walked up to the steps at Gabels Hus. The building, which was the rest of the year covered in ivy, was still beautiful in the winter. She walked inside and felt like she had entered someone's private house.

'Can I help you with anything?' a voice was behind her. She turned around. Christine realised it was probably not very common to walk around there in a ballgown at midnight when she wasn't a guest.

'I'm waiting for a guest of yours. Is it okay if I have a drink in the lounge while I wait?' she asked in her nicest possible voice.

'Of course, miss. Just tell the bartender in the lounge what you'd prefer.'

Christine sank down into one of the suede lounge chairs in front of the fire. She closed her eyes and breathed. She could not believe the night she had had. She had known it would be difficult for her to be at the party, but she'd had no idea that all of this would unfold. As the bartender brought her the white Russian she'd ordered, she received a message from Heidi. Christine smiled. *At least I have one vivid supporter for a reconciliation between Charlie and me.*

How did it go?

It went pretty badly, Christine replied to Heidi. **I am now acting desperate and waiting in case he appears at the hotel. I**

can't believe I am doing this.

Heidi quickly replied: **In an equal relationship, both people have to do crazy things.**

Christine smiled. This was the side of Heidi that no one saw, the smart, reflective side, the person that gave her advice when she needed it, and was able to listen.

That might be true, but I don't know what to do when he walks in here with that Jenny girl.

I took your goodie bag. Can't believe you forgot all of that free shit. It's true what they say, you have indeed gotten used to the high life. Do you want company while waiting? Haven't seen her with him for a while BTW.

Christine quickly replied.

Regarding goodie bag stealing, knock yourself out. Regarding the insane act of desperation, I need to do this by myself to show him which level of desperation I'm at.

Christine looked at her watch. Where was he? Charlie never stayed for afterparties, but that might have changed with Jenny. Christine went out to the reception area again.

'Excuse me, sir. I wasn't completely honest with you earlier. I am waiting for one of your guests, but he doesn't know that I am waiting for him. I was just wondering if you could double-check for me that he really is staying here? He is British, and is most likely staying here with his British girlfriend.' Christine knew that all embarrassment was now gone.

'We cannot give out information about our guests, miss.'

'I see. So, you can't tell me whether Mr. Charlie Lawson is staying here tonight?'

'I cannot, miss,' he said politely.

'I understand,' Christine said quietly, with disappointment written all over her face.

He smiled compassionately at her, and continued. "What I can tell you is that we have no guest with any *common English name* here tonight, nor have we had *that name* as a guest for a while.'

'Oh,' Christine knew that although the receptionist tried to help her, it didn't help at all. 'Do you know where *a common English name* might stay instead?'

'I know a *common English name* once talked about finding a place of their own.'

'Oh,' Christine knew this might have been a year ago, when he was working in Oslo. 'Thanks anyway,' Christine said disappointingly as she left. She put her coat on and stopped halfway out to the street. She stood there, wondering if she should go somewhere else to look for Charlie, but she had no idea where to go. She was wondering if she could find out where he was staying, but she couldn't think of whom she might ask in the middle of the night.

Instead, she looked up in the sky, and let the snowflakes fall on her face.

The Snowflake Catching

As she stood there looking up to the sky, Christine opened her mouth so her tongue would catch a few snowflakes. She remembered how as a child she would forget to walk home from school when the first snow arrived because she was too preoccupied with catching snowflakes with her mouth. It was so peaceful, the silence of the first snow, and the dance of the snowflakes.

Her gaze followed a snowflake to the ground. The new snow had covered all the gravel laid on top to prevent people from slipping. Everything on the ground was white; even the street was covered in the purest snow. She started to walk while she was chasing snowflakes. She went to catch one, and then took a step forward to catch another.

All of a sudden she noticed a couple, kissing close to the next crossing. Christine walked further, and she could not believe her eyes. *Was that Alex? Again?* She knew Alex lived close by, so it was natural he was in that area. *Who is that girl he is kissing?* Then she noticed a familiar shawl peeping up from the collar of the coat. *It's Jenny!* Christine couldn't help but smile and felt relief. At least Charlie and Jenny weren't in love, or at least Jenny wasn't in love with Charlie.She walked across the street, so they wouldn't notice her. When she got around the corner, she decided to take a detour home, so she wouldn't run into them again.

She started to chase snowflakes again, as she felt they might be her good-luck activity. It had certainly improved her night to be chasing them. They started to fall more intensely, and she started to feel a bit stressed to catch serveral. Suddenly, she noticed at the corner of her eye, that someone was watching her. A shadow came across the pavement, and stopped. The warm streetlight must have been far away, because the shadow was extremely long and narrow, but the man who created the shadow was perfect. He was formally dressed, with a dark coat and lacquered shoes, a complete nightmare on the snow. Not only did snow of any kind ruin shoes like that, but it was impossible for anyone to keep their balance with them on any sort of snow. When her gaze came to rest upon the man's face, she was already sure it was Charlie. He smiled at her. She didn't know what to say. She stood there for a few seconds. All she could think to say was:

'You have been here every week for three years, and you still haven't bought galoshes?'

Charlie laughed. 'I forgot them at the dinner. I wasn't thinking straight. How many snowflakes have you caught? She walked up to him and stopped a few steps away. 'I don't know. I lost count at least thirty snowflakes ago.. I have chased them since Gabels hus. I thought I might run into you there.'

'So … Do you want to get a drink? For old time's sake?' Charlie asked.

'I would love to,' she answered quickly.

'Where is the nearest bar?'

She smiled before she replied, 'I know this very nice little place. It's tiny and pretty cosy. They have a piano, actually. They will let you play, if you're any good.'

'That sounds nice.'

'It's just a few minutes down the road and across the street.' She nodded her head in the right direction.

'Just before we go, I just want to say I am still mad at you,

you know.'

'I know, and I understand,' she said.

The Piano Bar

They walked in the middle of the street, as the pavement was too slippery for Charlie's shoes to get a grip on. He tried to keep a cool attitude, but it wasn't easy. Their footsteps in the snow were so far apart you would think they were carrying something heavy between them. None of them dared to walk close to the other. Charlie followed Christine through a small garden and a beautiful old door. It was even more quiet than in the street, as the snow muted down all sounds.

'Is there really a bar in here?' he asked.

'Yes, it is a very tiny place,' she said with a smile. He nodded and followed her. As they walked up the old staircase, he made a sound of sudden realisation. It seemed that he knew where she was taking him. As she was looking for her keys, he said, 'Is it yours?'

'Yes, I have had this place for almost a year now, with a loan and everything.' She smiled proudly at him.

'Very nice,' he said as he entered the flat.

'Thank you. I was once at this great townhouse in London, my dream house, really, and I wanted to create the same atmosphere here, though it is a fraction of the size.' Charlie just smiled at her. He walked around, not saying anything. He looked at the books, and he looked at the pictures in the hall. As he walked into the living room, he passed a pair of ballet shoes lying on top of a bag on the floor.

'You've started dancing again?'

She just nodded. Then he saw the piano.

'Wow. You bought this too, or was it here?'

'Yes. You know, I had this dream that I would start to play, but then after a while I thought maybe I would find someone who could play it instead.'

Charlie sat down at the piano with his coat still on. He then touched a single note a few times. Christine bit her lip. She couldn't quite fathom that he was in her home.

'So, can I get you a drink? I don't have a great selection, but I do have a bottle of cognac or a bottle of cheap white wine if you fancy' she said nervously. Charlie started to touch a few more keys.

'I have to say Cognac now, don't I, to have some dignity after too many almost-accidents on my slippery shoes on our way here.'

She went into the kitchen, and as she poured two glasses, she heard that he had started playing a few more notes of a song. He wasn't singing, but she could hear him humming. Christine sat down next to him on the long piano seat and put his drink on top of the piano. She took a sip of her glass and hoped he wouldn't notice her trembling hand. He had taken off his coat and untied his bowtie. Something had fallen out of his pocket, and she picked it up.

'I'll take that,' he said very seriously, which made her even more curious, as it was obviously something he didn't want to show her. She managed to open it without him grabbing it. It was a note in his handwriting.

Subjects to talk about:

Christmas holiday

New Year's Eve

The Christmas concert last year

Favourite outings in Oslo

Is she with Henrik?

Suggest a work coffee during the weekend

It was a list of subjects to talk about for the lunch they had at

Colbert a year ago. His face had turned flashing red.

'You made a note in advance, so you had things to talk about with me?' Christine couldn't hide her smile as she asked him.

'You weren't supposed to see that. It was just in case it got awkward.'

She couldn't believe it. Charlie really had been as nervous as he seemed that day.

He looked down at the keys, but had stopped playing. She sat close to him, and she could feel he was tense.

'It was when I still had hope,' he admitted. Christine felt a rush of guilt and wondered how she could fix it. She leaned forward and kissed him on the side of his mouth. He turned to her, and kissed her back, properly.

'I am so sorry,' she said. 'But I had to do this.' She looked around the room. 'I had to do this in my own time for me, you see.'

'In a way, I am glad you did.'

'I was secretly hoping I would see you tonight. I do think I believed the lie Alex said to me, so I would have an excuse to just take a break for a while. It was all so intense, and so many things happened at once. I needed this year for myself.'

'I had heard that you weren't with Henrik anymore, and I slowly started to get my hopes up, but when I didn't hear from you, I felt you crushed me all over again. I through I was moving on, but I guess I went to the dinner this year because I had a hope you would show up tonight.'

'You did bring someone …'

'Well, I did maybe want you to feel a little bit jealous, just a tiny bit of what I felt. I am embarrassed to say I have never been so envious of anyone before, and I really didn't like myself like that. I am so sorry that I was a part of your breakup. I am sorry for you, and sorry for me about that. It was doomed from the start. I don't really believe any good relationships should start that way.'

'Well, I did my best this year to be the girl you would like to have met. Those talks we had, I think they really helped me to understand that I am good enough on my own. At the same time, I realised I shouldn't be with someone who doesn't really want to be with me.'

'Well, I'm glad you got your own place.' Charlie looked at her with his open and innocent looking brown eyes.

'Now I hope this guy I am quite into won't mind spending some time here,' she said. He looked surprised, so she leaned in and kissed him.

'Don't break my heart again,' he whispered. She moved closer to him.

The Text from Harald

Christine woke up in his arms. It was still dark, and she couldn't believe Charlie was in her bed. She was with the guy who she had dreamt about for *years*, and then had realised was as amazing as she once had thought. He was in her bed, and she didn't have one guilty thought about it. It felt great. She kissed his cheek and lay her head at his chest again.

*

She woke up again. It was still dark. She turned around to lie closer to Charlie, but he must have moved further away. She opened one eye. He wasn't there. Christine listened to see if she could hear him in the bathroom, but she couldn't hear a sound. She turned around and lifted her head from the pillow, so she could see the bathroom door. It was open, and the lights were off. He wasn't there.

'Charlie?'

There was no response.

Is this really happening? Has he left? Christine couldn't believe it. *Was this all revenge?* No, Christine didn't want to believe the worst this time. *Was he having cold feet? Didn't he know that Jenny had been with Alex?* Christine found her watch. It was 7:30. She dressed quickly, and ran outside.

*

She had to speak to him. She had to make him realise that she was serious about them, just as he had been. She tried to call him but both times, there was no answer. Maybe he had regretted the night with her? That he had realised he was still mad? As she ran outside, Christine remembered that she hadn't asked him where he was staying. It was 7.30… Who could she ask where he was staying? Would Heidi know? No, she would definitely be asleep, and the chances she would reply were minimal. Maybe Harald? He was up at 6 am every day. She started texting.

Thanks for a great party last night and thank you for your good advice. Would you happen to know where Charlie is staying in Oslo?

It took a few seconds before a reply beeped in.

Glad you enjoyed yourself. I believe it is through the first

doorway in Haxhausens gate from Frognerveien.

Another text came pretty quickly.

Good luck!

Can't be a hotel then. It only took her a few minutes to get to Haxhausens gate. *Okay, the first gate ... can this be it?* She looked a wooden gate in a light blue facade. It was ajar. She looked through. *Can I just walk in?* She took a quick look at the names on the calling system. There were no names she recognised. She gently pushed the gate open and walked inside. There were traces of snow in there, as if someone had just walked through into the courtyard. She followed the steps and saw lights on at a little cottage in the backyard. The cottage was in red plaster with white details. It looked like it had just been renovated, and she could see from the outside that it was pretty nice inside. She walked closer, maybe she could see if Charlie was inside. She was crossing her fingers that Jenny wouldn't be there. Someone in a red jacket was walking around inside. *It does look a lot like Charlie...* Christine walked closer to the door and was ready to press the bell. Right before she had gathered the strength she needed to go ahead, the door quickly opened. Christine almost screamed. Charlie was also not prepared for anyone to be there, and by the look of his face, he was quite surprised.

'Hi…' he said.

'Please don't leave! I love you, Charlie. I think I have been in love with you for a very long time. Not only are you the most attractive person I have ever met, but I don't think I have ever met anyone who felt as much my best friend as you, which is a pretty amazing thing.'

Charlie smiled at her with his perfect smile. 'I left you a note saying I would be back in fifteen minutes.'

'I didn't see that. I thought you regretted everything, and wanted to get back with Jenny.' Christine was a bit embarrassed by her outburst and tried to hide her face in her coat.

'Jenny was pretty preoccupied with Alex last night.' He explained.

'Yes.. I saw that too.. but I didn't know if you knew that.'

'I knew and I saw them. I guess I can't blame her, it's not like I gave her any attention at all last night, and we're not dating, never have.'

'But didn't I see her shawl at yours last year?'

'She has never been to my house. That must have been my sister's shawl.'

Christine smiled relieved.

'On my way over here, I saw Alex, naked in the street. She must have kicked him out or something.'

'We maybe should have told her he is a jerk.'

'Maybe, but it was a pretty funny sight on a morning stroll.'

'Why *did* you take a morning stroll?'

'This is my place, actually.'

'Really?' She couldn't believe no one had told her that.

'I bought it last year, since I would be spending time here with the start-up. I should have told you, but I didn't want to brag about it last night, since having your own space was a pretty big thing for you. I just left to buy some coffee and baked goods for us, and then I remembered that you once said you couldn't date someone you had almost only seen in a dinner jacket, so I just stopped by to pick up some more casual clothes.'

It was silent for a moment. She didn't know what to say.

'You've really bought a place here?'

'Yes, I did,' he smiled. 'And about that other thing, I want to be with you too, since I think I am in love with you.'

Christine sighed with relief.

"Can I kiss you?" She stepped towards him.

A great smile appeared on his face. She leaned in. She could smell him, she wanted that moment to last forever. He tucked his arms around her. She grabbed his chin, and kissed him.

About the author

S.J. Thompson has been living most of her life in Oslo, Norway, with periods in the United Kingdom, United States and Denmark. With a degree in the Arts, from University of Edinburgh and Aarhus, she also took up creative writing, and kept it as a side business next to her job at Scandinavian creative firm, where she is partner. She currently lives in Oslo with her husband and daughter.

Sign up for discount on next book:
https://www.sjthompson.net/about

Printed in Great Britain
by Amazon